CW01496526

SPELL, DON'T TELL

THE ACCIDENTAL MEDIUM BOOK THREE

AMY BOYLES

LADYBUGBOOKS LLC

CHAPTER 1

J first realized my sister and I would never be friends the night she confessed to stealing money from the mob.

Here was the thing: when your eyes were glued to a gym bag over-flowing—*correction, vomiting*—one-hundred-dollar bills, were you supposed to rejoice with glee?

You were if the money was legitimate.

But this situation was far from aboveboard.

"Cammie, what have you done?"

I stared at my sister. She tried to run fingers through her black teased-up hair, but that cobweb of tresses was glued together tightly. She grimaced and her shoulders sank in, making her look small. A gusty sigh rushed from her lungs, and she peered up at me with an apology in her eyes.

"I'm sorry?"

I closed my lids in frustration and pinched the bridge of my nose. "Are you asking me if you're sorry or telling me?"

"Both," she squeaked.

My lids snapped open. "Where did all this money come from? You're broke, remember? Using my money to fund your picnics with leprechauns."

A tiny frown line appeared between her brows. "Leprechauns?"

"Never mind."

Perhaps I should hit the brakes and back up. My name is Paige Provey, and I'm a middle-aged witch with little control of my gift. That's not even the most important detail right now as my sister, who is *also* middle-aged (in fact, she's older than me and should know better) appeared at the cottage I was staying at a few days ago and has been mooching off me ever since. We'd just buried the hatchet we'd held against one another for our entire lives when I discovered in her possession a gym bag filled with money. It was so stuffed it reminded me of a twice-baked potato bursting with cheese and potato guts.

"Where did this cash come from?" I demanded.

Snow, my resident phantom, floated over from the kitchenette and raked her opaque fingers across the money. She studied it with an eye cocked in curiosity. "There's so much. You could rent a bigger cabin, Paige."

Was no one but me concerned about the origins of said cash? "Cammie, if you don't tell me right now, I'm kicking you out of this cabin tonight."

Cammie's eyes brimmed with tears. "Okay, I'll tell you. I was dating this guy who may or may not have been involved with the mob."

Cold dread seeped into my chest. "Are you telling me that he was?"

She lifted one shoulder and tipped her head in apology. "He may have been."

I exhaled and dropped onto the couch. I scraped my fingernails over my scalp, letting them bite into my flesh. The pain felt good. It actually felt more real than this crazy train of a night I was on.

When I looked up, Cammie had her nose tipped to the ceiling and was staring at it as if she were an innocent victim of a stowaway duffel bag filled with dirty money.

"Start at the beginning," I told her.

Snow floated over and sat by me. She tucked a strand of blonde hair behind an ear and gracefully crossed one leg over the other. She entwined her delicate fingers, placing them on her knee, and watched Cammie with all the attention of an enraptured socialite.

"I would love to hear it," she said.

"It all started when I met Newman, that SOB," Cammie started.

"Oh, I knew a Newman once," Snow told us eagerly. "He was tall, dark and handsome." Her nose wrinkled as if from recalling a troubling memory. "But Newman would sometimes disappear, and then in his place, there would be a dark spot in the sky."

I patted her hand in sympathy. "I'm pretty sure you're confusing memories of Superman with your actual life."

She touched her cherry-red lips. "No, I don't think so."

Yes, I think so. I turned back to Cammie. "Keep going."

Cammie dug through her purse and pulled out a pack of gum. She lifted it in offering, but I turned her down. She unwrapped a stick and shoved it into her mouth, real ladylike.

She spoke through obnoxious smacking. "Well, Newman was all charming and loving at first, and he always had wads of cash—I mean big fistfuls." She lifted her hands in the shape of claws holding invisible money. "We had a great time until I caught his butt cheating on me."

Snow shook her head sadly. "Isn't that the way it always goes? They're wonderful until they're cheating on you." Her gaze darted to the ground. "Yes, that's how it is."

"Snow, do you remember something?"

"No, I don't think so." She paused before a big bubbly laugh tinkled from her throat. "I was just going on about nonsense. Don't mind me."

I watched her carefully for a moment. Snow didn't recall much from her life as a human, other than that she'd lived in Willow Lake, where I was currently vacationing to recharge my nonexistent writing career after being canceled and humiliated on national television. But instead I was entertaining my thief of a sister and hanging out with ghosts.

You could see how my life was going.

"What happened with Newman?" I asked my sister.

Cammie wretched and spit the gum into her hand. She tossed it into a trash can, mumbling, "Lost its dang flavor after only two seconds. I ain't ever buying that crap again."

"Newman?" I impatiently reminded her. "What happened?"

"Oh, right." She brushed her hands on her thighs. "Well, I caught his butt cheating on me at the hoedown bar and so I broke into his truck and stole this here duffel bag." She patted the money proudly.

So much to unpack in that sentence. Hoedown bar? She broke into his truck? I decided to push on rather than request details. "Did you know what was in the bag at the time?"

"Nuh-uh. No clue. But I found out when I got it home and opened it."

My heart seized like the hand of death had reached into my chest and squeezed it. "And you came here? You didn't return it? Newman may not have even known it was stolen."

Cammie clicked her tongue in triumph. "Oh, he knew. I smashed out the back window. There was no ignoring that."

Jeez.

She continued, this time in a more somber voice. "When I got home and peeked inside was when I figured out that I was up a creek without a paddle. I suspected that Newman wasn't on the up-and-up, and then the money proved it. I was so proud of myself for listening to my instincts." She tapped her temple smugly. "I'm a real smartie."

My eye twitched. I was unknowingly housing drug or blood money, and she was *proud* of herself? I swallowed several deep gulps of air and told myself we could figure this out.

I rose and paced the claustrophobically tiny room. "Okay, we can fix this."

"Oh, there ain't no fixing it," my sister murmured.

"*Cammie*," I screeched. She jumped in fear. "This is not the time to contradict me. We, you and me—"

"And me," Snow offered.

My eyes snapped in her direction. "You do not count. You are a ghost." I inhaled another gulp of air and closed my eyes, trying to think. "Okay. We've got to return the money."

"No can do."

My lids flipped open. "What do you mean, *no can do?*"

Cammie scoffed. "What am I supposed to do? Call my cheating ex-boyfriend and tell him I've got his money?"

"Yes." The word exploded from my mouth. "That's exactly what you're supposed to do. Cammie, how could you have been so childish? You're my older sister. You're supposed to make good decisions, not bad ones."

She shrugged as if it was no big deal. As if no one would track down a bag stuffed full of cash and kill whoever had stolen it.

"It'll be fine," she insisted.

I marched over to the bag, shoved my fist inside and closed my hand around a wad of cash. When I pulled it out, wrapped bills cascaded down my arm and plopped onto the floor. I thrust the fistful of cash under her nose.

"It will not be fine. Newman or his boss will come looking for this, and when they discover that both of us know about the money, they will kill us. Do you understand?"

Her gaze cut to the floor. "But Newman's nice."

"Not when it comes to this, he's not. Cammie, I don't care what you have to do, but within two days I want this money gone. I want it out of here, and I want to be alive and well."

When she looked up at me, her eyes glistened with tears. "But he'll kill me for stealing it."

So Cammie knew. Of course she did. My sister's whole we'll-be-fine display was only an act. I sighed and slumped onto the couch. I opened my fingers, and the cash poured back onto the duffel.

I dropped my forehead into my hands. "You came here as soon as you discovered the money, didn't you?"

"Yes," she whispered.

"And you haven't spent one dime of it, have you?"

"No." I heard her gulp. "Paige, what are we gonna do?"

First of all, I nearly spat, *it's not we, it's you.* "Call Newman. Arrange a meeting."

Her voice thinned. "Where?"

I sighed and slumped back onto the couch. "Out on the lake, some-place secluded."

"I know just the spot," Snow offered.

She told us about it, and I nodded. "That sounds perfect—easy to find but remote. Tell Newman that."

"And what about the gun he'll be bringing? Or the other men who'll be ready for us?"

"Leave that to me."

One side of her mouth curved into a smile. "You gonna call that hottie Grim to help?"

"No, I am not going to call that hottie Grim. I have my own plan. Or I'll have one by then. Listen, don't worry about that. I'll come up with something."

Cammie watched me cautiously. She knew that I saw ghosts, but she

5

didn't know the rest—that I possessed powers with a life of their own. Between now and my meeting with Newman, I needed a quick and dirty method of using magic that would scare the mob off Cammie for good. So that she'd never have to worry about them retaliating.

Grim would help, I knew. But our relationship was too young, too fragile for me to call him and announce I was in trouble with the mob. Pretty sure we'd never survive that blow.

No. I had a better idea than dragging him into this.

"I'll call Newman," Cammie said suddenly, shoving the money deep into the mouth of the duffel and zipping it tight. "Tomorrow. And then we'll meet up." She slung the bag over her shoulder and mumbled, "I'm sorry, Paige. For all of it—appearing on your doorstep, for stealing your money to buy groceries, and for lying."

I couldn't spit out a thank-you or even an, *I forgive you.* By appearing on my doorstep, Cammie had yanked me into this madness. She had dragged me into a relationship with the mob, one I'd never asked for.

As soon as this was over and the money returned, I'd give my sister a hug and show her the door, shoving her over the threshold if need be. How could I trust her after this? After she jeopardized my life?

We were different people—Cammie lived on the fringes, a life of surviving month to month, of loving men fiercely and then collapsing when those relationships crumbled into flaming piles of dog poop only weeks later.

I was the opposite—weighing the pros and cons of situations as if they were the scales of justice. I pondered over consequences before leaping into decisions, and I certainly didn't date men with thoughtless abandon. Being recently divorced did that to a person.

Take Grim, for instance. We have off-the-charts chemistry. How could we not with his wavy dark hair, eyes that glinted like gemstones, and his muscular body kissed with golden sky. Let me rephrase that, how could *I* not have chemistry with him?

We do. *I* do. But the last time we found our bodies touching and my fingernails scraping over his back, he basically said that he promised himself he would never get too attached to a woman. Even though he confessed that, one-half of me wanted to ignore his words and give myself to him totally.

But what a blow that would be to my psyche. I couldn't survive being emotionally crushed right now. And I would be if I handed the keys to my heart to him (along with my body) and after he turned that key, he then tossed it over his shoulder, where it plunged off a cliff.

My chest tightened just thinking about that.

But back to Cammie.

As she slid the bag into a closet with her foot, shoving it in until it couldn't be seen (yes, still with her toe), the knowledge that we'd never be friends hit me.

We were sisters, but we would never be anything else. We were too different, unable to understand one another. I would help her become untangled from this mess, but after the duffel bag was back with Newman, I would show my sister the door.

Cammie plopped back on top of the couch, and she pulled the throw blanket up to her chin and nested it between her legs. "So. What do we do now?"

I handed her my phone. "Now you call Newman. Not tomorrow. *Now*."

CHAPTER 2

urned out, Newman didn't answer. His voice mail hadn't been set up, and with no way to leave a message, Cammie hung up. We didn't talk about it anymore until the next night, when I was pushing hoop earrings into my ears.

"Where you going?" she asked, her voice ringing with accusation.

"A…date with Grim. Why? Is there something wrong?"

She tossed her hands up. "I thought you were going to hang around to protect me, make sure nothing happened."

"Cammie, you've tried to call Newman a few times. I can't stay here twenty-four-seven. Besides, you've got a gun." I nodded to her purse. "You've got protection."

She nibbled her bottom lip. "Maybe I'll call Ferguson."

"No," I nearly screeched. "You can't bring him over here."

The last time that my sister and the leprechaun (she didn't know that) had gotten cozy at my house, I'd been nearly blinded by the tangle of naked limbs that I'd walked in on.

"I was only going to invite him over to watch a movie," she said, her lips pouting. "I haven't seen him in days."

My heart softened. "All right. Fine. But you're only watching a movie. There's not to be any hanky-panky."

She lifted her hand like she was taking an oath. "I swear. No hanky-panky."

The doorbell rang and I shoved my clutch under my arm. "How do I look?"

I took a quick peek in the mirror, not fully trusting Cammie's opinion. After all, her graying locks were dyed inky black.

My bangs were swept to one side, revealing the fine lines that crept across my forehead. I pulled the hair down, trying to cover the wrinkles, but only succeeded in hiding about half of my face.

I really needed some Botox.

Other than the wrinkles that kept drawing my eye, I looked pretty good. The two layers of Spanx (just kidding—not really) smoothed my body in all the right places and made my dark leather pants do their job —to show off my curves.

I opened the door, and Grim stood in the doorway. My breath hitched at the sight of him. He was tall with wide shoulders and biceps hard as stone. His dark hair hung in waves that cascaded over his shoulders and his hazel eyes glinted like emeralds ringed in copper. He held out a hand and mine slid over his, the rough surface hewn with callouses.

"You look beautiful," he murmured in a husky voice.

Heat crept to my cheeks at the very sound of his low purr. "Thank you. So do you. Not beautiful. *Handsome*, I mean."

"Looking good, Grim," Cammie said, coming into view. "Take good care of my sister tonight, if you know what I mean."

I wasn't looking at her, but it wouldn't have surprised me if Cammie winked while making an obscene gesture with her hand. I wanted to slip through a wall like Snow and vanish.

I not so gently pushed Grim through the door. "Okay, we will. Bye, Cammie."

I shut the door behind me without looking back.

"So," I said as we walked outside. "Where are we going? And where's your bike?" I asked, glancing around in confusion.

"I got something easier for you to ride in." He pressed the fob in his hand, and a sleek sedan blinked to life. "What do you think?"

I ran a hand over the glossy surface. "Very nice. But you're more of a motorcycle guy to me. Look." I pointed to my pants. "I even dressed for it."

He chuckled. "Which is why I got this. Now you can wear dresses and not worry about tucking them in."

It was my turn to laugh. "I like sitting on my skirts."

He opened the door for me. "Why do I think you're lying?"

I shrugged. "I'm not."

I stopped in front of him. Our gazes locked and I studied him for a long heartbeat, my eyes drinking in the details of his face—the small dimple on his cheek that only peeked out when he laughed, how the corners of his eyes crinkled in delight, the small mole by his right ear.

He leaned forward and brushed his lips against mine, sending flames licking down my spine.

"I like you, Paige," he whispered.

"I like you, too." I wound my fingers around his neck and drew him in for another kiss. *Why wasn't I throwing myself at him again?* I wondered as he parted his lips and the kiss deepened. Oh right, because I didn't want to be hurt.

But I was only living in Willow Lake for a few months. I could manage a little fling. It wouldn't kill me to live dangerously for once. Maybe living a little like Cammie would be a good thing.

Until I wound up with a duffel bag overflowing with drug or blood money, that was.

When we finally untangled and were both inside the car, I said, "Where are you taking me tonight?"

He lifted a coy eyebrow. "To the fair."

THE COUNTY FAIR had arrived in Willow Lake only a few days prior. As my current situation meant that I was tangled up with Cammie and her drama, I had completely missed the announcement, along with the flyers pinned up around town and the large swath of field that the fair sat on.

Children dashed around us while teenagers moseyed about the stalls of food. Every food station advertised what it sold in bright, bold letters and pictures. There was the fried vegetable stand, the pizza place decorated in red and orange, the fried dessert box, the hamburger store with blue and white streamers shooting from its roof to the ground, where they were hammered down.

"Wow, there are a lot of fried foods here," I murmured.

Grim winked. "I won't judge if you want them."

I chuckled. "How about we tackle some rides?"

"Sure thing."

After thirty minutes of experiencing my stomach dropping at least one hundred times and my neck tight from traveling at breakneck speeds, I was ready for a breather. Grim purchased a roasted turkey leg for us to split.

"What? No cotton candy?" I joked.

His gaze cut away from his plate and latched on to me, sending a chill wrapping down my spine. "Darling, you can have whatever you'd like."

Talk about getting the tingles! I bit down the desire building up in my body and focused on the food. The meat was seasoned perfectly, and it was so tender that it fell off the bone.

"I've never come here before," Grim said as his gaze roamed the crowd.

"What? You don't bring all your dates here?" I teased.

Darkness flashed in his eyes. "No, I don't."

Had I said something wrong? "I'm sorry, I didn't mean to offend you."

"You didn't." His gaze softened and one side of his mouth lifted in a slight smile. "You're the first woman I've dated in a long time."

My jaw nearly fell to the table. "But you can have any woman you want."

He shrugged. "And you can have any man."

So he thought. "I just figured you'd dated more."

His gaze roved the crowd, his eyes distant. "Not since my last girl-friend almost killed me. I haven't wanted to." His attention was on me now. "It takes a lot for me to give my heart to someone."

The earnest look in his eyes made a knot form in my throat. He wasn't calling me his girlfriend, was he? Hadn't he told me previously that he couldn't commit? He had. I remembered it.

I wiped my grease-coated fingers on my napkin. "I know all about handing a heart over. It does take a lot, because who wants to be hurt? No one. And you know, I'm only here temporarily, so no worries."

Was that pain flashing in his eyes? If it was, it vanished as quickly as it flared.

"We've both been hurt," Grim told me. "We're wounded people, Paige."

I lifted my bottle of water. "To being wounded."

He toasted with his water and nodded. "Yes." When I settled the bottle back on the table, Grim traced his fingers over mine. Heat snaked up my wrist. "But how do we heal?"

I wasn't looking at him, and when I dared to, the heat smoldering in his gaze lit me on fire. The intensity of his stare shriveled my voice to a squeak. "Heal?"

He nodded. "You can't stay wounded forever. Not when there's so much fried food to eat."

I burst into laughter, and when it died down in my throat, I found his gaze still searching me, waiting for an answer. "Well, I suppose to heal, one has to decide to heal. To open their heart."

He nodded slightly as his fingers worked their way up to my wrist. "Go on."

"And"—it was impossible to focus on words when his fingers were making swirl marks on my skin—"you also have to be with someone whose heart is open, too."

"Yes," he purred.

Was it legal for him to touch me like this in public? He was only stroking my wrist, but I felt every ounce of my flesh tingle—even the hidden parts. I licked my lips, and his eyes flicked down to watch.

Have to concentrate. "And then when you're with someone whose heart is open, same as yours, you give each other permission to learn from the other. Everyone has wounds. All of us are broken in some way. It takes coming together and knowing what sort of contract you're signing with the other before you can start to mend."

"Equal footing," he clarified.

"Right. You have to be on equal footing."

Now his fingers slid up to my elbow as he tugged me just a little bit closer. "I would like for us to be on equal footing."

What did *that* mean? "I came from a messy family. My mom worked two jobs to feed and clothe us. Cammie was a bossy older sister, and we were never close. Soon as I could, I left. Then I met Walter. We were on equal footing for a long time, or I thought so. We couldn't have children. I wanted them, but he seemed indifferent. He wasn't always bad, not like he became in the end. He didn't always spy on our neighbors while they changed clothes. But maybe," I sighed, "maybe now that I think about, maybe we weren't on equal footing. My work was my life. Perhaps he needed more from me—something that I didn't even know I was supposed to give."

"No," Grim growled. "He made his own decisions. Walter was a fool to have treated you the way that he did. You are a light. You are my muse, Paige."

It felt like a coil in my stomach snapped apart. One that I didn't even know existed. "Your muse?"

A seductive smile quirked his lips. "I haven't felt anything for a long time, not for someone. I haven't let myself. But you've worked your way into my mind."

"I have?" I whispered.

We were finished eating, and he rose, taking my hand. He led me through the fair. Laughter and lights blurred into the background because the only thought roaming about my head was that Grim had called me his muse. I was his muse. How had that happened?

And what did that mean?

We piled into his sedan, and I was silent as he drove. "I'd been working on something for a long time," he told me. "But I could never quite figure it out."

Streetlamps glowing with amber light whizzed past. Trees and houses melted into the night as Grim whipped us around curves.

"Could never figure what out?"

"You'll see."

We reached his house, and Grim opened my door. He took me by the hand and pulled me gently inside as he explained. "I have my greenhouse, as you know, but it has limits of the creatures it can hold and what it can do. I wanted to expand it, but I didn't know how until I met you."

We were inside now and standing before the door. His winged dog,

Savage, padded up and pushed his nose under my hand. I gave his silky head a pat, and Grim ran his thumb across my cheek.

"Close your eyes."

I did as he said, and I heard the creaking of a door as it opened. The smell of earth and vegetation trickled up my nose, and I felt the humidity of water dancing over my skin. I even thought that I heard the sound of it splashing, too.

Grim's mouth was to my ear. My head became foggy, drunk off his earthy scent as he murmured, "Okay, open your eyes."

CHAPTER 3

I opened my eyes and sucked air. Grim's greenhouse looked like it had the first time I'd ever entered—panes of frosty leaded glass apexed into a sharply arched ceiling above us. Midway up the walls were light sconces that cast a warm glow on the room. Lining the walls on either side were plants overflowing with thick green leaves that snaked along the floor like giant emerald tongues. Unseen creatures chirped from within the foliage.

But way in the back towering above us, fell a waterfall. It was created from nothing, there was no river feeding it, but yet it existed—a freestanding wall of water that plunged into a pool. From it rose steam that curled to the ceiling.

My jaw unhinged with disbelief. "You *made* this?"

He strode forward, shooting me a passing glance over his shoulder. "I made it for you."

"For me?"

I caught up to him, and Grim took my hand. He turned to me and brushed a strand of hair from my face. "I've spent a long time hiding my heart. I don't want to do that anymore."

My ears drank in his words. "Um, okay." Wow, for a writer I had a lot to learn about witty responses. "So, what do you mean?"

"I mean…" His fingers traced over my ear. His kissable lips parted as if he were about to say something, and then he paused before confessing, "I enjoy spending time with you."

Was that all? My heart deflated. Grim was supposed to say that he didn't want us to be casual, that he was ready to throw his heart at me with abandon. "I enjoy spending time with you, too. But you looked as if you were about to say more."

Darkness clouded his eyes. "I have a dangerous job."

"Hunting monsters," I filled in for him.

"Doing that." He stared at the pool for a long moment, his eyes becoming distant. "I don't want you to be hurt because of me."

I clicked my tongue in mock arrogance. "I don't know if you've noticed, but I'm an expert witch."

He threw back his head and laughed. "You are far from that."

"I know." The only sound for a moment was the chirping creatures and the falling water as it broke against the pool's surface. "But you don't have to protect me."

He watched me for a moment before his gaze cut to the water. He eyed the pool mischievously. "Care for a swim?"

"I didn't bring my suit," I replied, a chill wrapping around my heart because Grim had simply said that he enjoyed spending time with me. Who builds a waterfall for someone they casually like?

But Grim's warm hands wrapped around my neck, and the hardness that threatened to settle into me softened. How could I be angry with him for telling me the truth? How could I be mad when Grim was giving me all that he could? After all, his last girlfriend (if I dared call myself such) had tried to kill him and, in doing so, had left a nasty scar tracing down his back.

He pulled me to him and softly kissed my lips, then my nose, each cheek, and the soft spot underneath my jaw.

"I don't have a suit, either. But I'll only leave on what's comfortable."

I shivered under his touch. When we parted, I was drunk off his presence, off his kisses, off him. I backed away. "Don't look."

He turned around, hands up in surrender, giving me a view of his delicious backside. "I promise not to look."

I undressed to my bra and panties (the spanks were a pain to slip out of) and jumped into the water. It was warm and silky, the water gliding over my body like a velvet blanket.

Grim left on his underwear, and I nearly choked on the sight of the muscles cut into his abdomen, of his flat belly, his taut thighs.

We swam and laughed, and I sprayed him with water. He splashed back, but gently, and we circled one another until I wound up in his arms.

"You inspired me to do this. Thank you, my muse."

"You're welcome," I replied, kissing him.

After a few minutes we pulled ourselves from the pool. Grim found towels and handed me one. It was pink.

"Why do you have a pink towel?" I asked.

"It's my sister's."

My eyes nearly popped from my head. "You have a sister? I didn't know that."

He stiffened. "She doesn't come around much."

The air seemed to contract, tightening around him. Though smoke still curled up from the pool, clouding the greenhouse, I swore that tiny sparks of lightning sparked off his skin. Okay, so maybe his sister wasn't a pleasant topic of conversation.

My phone rang and I saw that it was Cammie. My heart sank. For a few brief hours I'd been able to shove aside my worry about the money and the mob. But her name lighting up my cell phone was a sharp reminder of the potential trouble she was in—and me through proximity.

I frowned at the phone, and Grim's voice broke into my reverie. "Everything okay?"

"Yeah."

"Are you going to answer that?"

"No." His eyes narrowed in suspicion. "Yes, I mean." I thumbed the answer button and turned away from him. "Hey."

"Paige, I'm sorry to disturb y'all."

My heart thundered. Was Newman at the cabin? Had he tracked Cammie down and had a gun to her head?

"Everything okay?" I asked, breathless.

"Yes, it's just…"

Her voice trailed off, and worry jackknifed down my spine. "It's just what?"

"Abraham's here wondering if we need anything."

I exhaled a gusty sigh of relief. Abraham was my landlady, Patricia's, nephew. He was like twelve or something, and he got us groceries. Delivered them on his bike.

"I don't need anything, but tell Abraham to get home because it's late."

"Will do."

We hung up and I slipped the phone in my pants' pocket. "Everything okay?" Grim asked.

"Yes, it's fine."

His gaze scoured over my face, and I had the feeling that he was studying my expression to see if I was lying. I flashed him a smile. "Everything's good as gold."

He said nothing as he secured the towel around his waist. But I had the distinct feeling Grim knew I was lying, that I was holding something back. Just like I'd felt when he answered that he enjoyed spending time with me. Grim was lying, too.

But why?

THE NEXT MORNING my body still hummed with happiness from the night before. I was euphorically stupid, humming as I worked at the computer, trying to finish the novel that was due to my publisher.

I'd arrived at Willow Lake with a crippling case of writer's block and that was gone, but the effects of it still threatened to creep up every time I checked my Twitter feed. Reading things like *Paige Provey #fake* was not good for the soul.

But sometimes I looked anyway. In fact, I did just then, searching my name. Only a few folks were hating on me, typing *Paige Provey #totalliar.*

I sighed because my readers had believed that I was a liar because I made them think that I had the powers to see ghosts. The thing was, months ago I didn't. But now I did.

And I needed this new book to redeem my reputation.

Snow drifted into the living room while I was finishing a chapter. Cammie lay asleep on the couch. My sister slept the sleep of the dead;

nothing short of an atomic bomb explosion would lull her from dreamland.

"Have you talked to Patricia?" Snow asked in her singsong voice as she floated over to hover-sit on an empty chair.

"Drat, no I haven't! She knew Pam. I'll call her today and find out if she's back from Hawaii."

Snow slid her long, lithe fingers delicately through her golden hair. "Maybe Pam's still alive and we can find out what happened to me— why I was trapped in the book and killed in the first place."

My heart broke for Snow. Twenty years ago she'd been doing laundry, living the dream life of a housewife. Well, maybe. Snow didn't remember much about her husband or if she had children. Her mind was mostly blank.

But it was during those salad days of her life when Snow had been sucked into the book, *A Study in the Paranormal* by Heronomous Spell. It housed magical creatures—a couple of which had been unleashed on the town, or so Grim and I believed. That same book also ignited my latent witch abilities—abilities that I thought I should give a shot to right then.

I plucked my coffee cup from beside me on the table. It was frigid from neglect. I nestled it between my hands and focused on my magic. My power hitchhiked off other people's abilities, technically making me a magical succubus. Perhaps Grim's magic still mingled with my power. He could command lightening, and all that heat needed to go somewhere.

I peeked over my shoulder and saw that Cammie still slumbered. She'd fallen asleep with her face planted in the couch and hadn't moved since I'd been up.

I tightened my grip on the cup. Sparks clustered on my fingertips, and next thing I knew, steam curled from the inside of my cup. "So cool!"

"Where'd you learn that trick?" Snow asked.

I smiled proudly. "I just taught it to myself." I dropped my voice. "I called on Grim's power."

Snow stretched out her legs. "And how is Grim?"

"He's good. Built me a pool. Or I guess he built it for himself. But he called me his muse," I added with a note of wonder winding through my voice. "I've never been anyone's muse before."

Snow's eyes widened. "His muse! Oh my gosh, he likes you so much! He's falling hard, Paige."

I waved her away. "No, he's not. He isn't. He told me not too long ago that he didn't want to commit to anyone."

"Maybe he doesn't want to commit, but he certainly is gaga about you."

I hadn't thought about that. Grim didn't strike me as the type to simply hand over his heart, even though he'd said he didn't want to hide it anymore. But hiding and handing it over were two very different things.

My stomach knotted. Grim was gorgeous and in my experience, the more gorgeous a man, the more of a player they were. Was he playing me?

The knots in my tummy became coiled rope. I didn't want to think about this, but my mind churned like we were making ice cream the old-fashioned way—with a hand crank.

There was no way around it; Grim's actions clashed against his words. He couldn't commit—he'd said as much—but he was tired of hiding his heart. He'd built a pool, but he hadn't declared love.

Besides, it was too early for that anyway. We barely knew each other. Yet when we were together, I felt blissful, open and honest. His presence filled me with happiness. He left me full; even my magic could attest to that.

My head hurt from the overload of information. I shut my laptop, and with my warm coffee in hand, I rose and said to Snow, "Want to call Patricia?"

She nodded eagerly. "Yes, oh yes!"

With her face buried in a couch cushion, Cammie mumbled, "Do you know how annoying it is to hear only one side of a conversation?"

I cringed. "Sorry. I was trying to whisper."

She lifted her head. Thick smudges of mascara rimmed her eyes. "When you got to Grim, you stopped whispering. All I heard was how hot he is with those big muscles he's got."

I shook my head in confusion. "I didn't talk about his muscles."

She shrugged. "Must've imagined that."

I smiled. "I was just about to call Patricia and see if she could steer us toward Pam, Snow's old neighbor."

Cammie was up now, rubbing her eyes and streaking the mascara down toward her cheeks. "My date with Ferguson was great, thanks so much for asking. Yes, we had a wonderful time. He didn't pay thousands of dollars for someone to build him a pool, though."

Right. Cammie didn't know about my whole magic deal. Not too long ago, my sister had confessed that if she ever met a witch or wizard, she would kill them.

Yes, she embraced my ability to communicate with the dead. Apparently our grandmother had also possessed the gift. But magic and power, those were gigantic no-no's to Cammie. An abomination, she thought them to be.

So mum was the word on my magic. The safest topic of conversation with my sister was men. "Glad you had a good time with Ferguson."

She shoved herself off the couch. She'd slept with her hair in a bun. Now the tresses shot out like a handful of sticks in every direction. My sister patted the mess.

"Coffee," she mumbled as she stumbled into the kitchen area.

I slid my phone from a tabletop and flashed it at Snow. "Ready to call?"

She sat up eagerly. "Why, yes."

I dialed Patricia's number and crossed my fingers. After three rings, there was an answer. "Hello?"

I jabbed the button to put her on speaker. "Patricia, can you hear me?"

"Yes," my landlady answered in a gruff voice. "What do you need?"

My chest constricted. This was it. Snow was about to get her answers.

CHAPTER 4

*P*atricia spoke sharply. "Is the cabin on fire? Did an earthquake destroy it?"

"No," I said slowly. "Why?"

"Because it's four a.m. here in Hawaii."

I cringed. "I'm so sorry. I didn't mean to wake you, but this is important."

"Hang on a second."

I heard shuffling and Patricia muttering to someone that she had to take the call and why couldn't I have dialed at a decent hour. The whole time my face burned with embarrassment.

I flashed a brilliant smile at Snow. This was just a little bump; that was all it was.

"Maybe we should call back," she whispered, even though Patricia couldn't hear her.

"No, it's fine," I lied.

Patricia's voice snapped back onto the line, loud and clear. "Okay, what is it that's so important? What couldn't Abraham handle?"

"This has nothing to do with the cabin."

A long stretch of silence followed, and I quickly realized my mistake. First rule of renting—do not awaken your burly landlady while she's on vacation seeing how things go with the Internet friend who could turn out to be the love of her life.

"What is it?" she growled.

"There's a woman in town named Pam. She used to live out in a subdivision along the lake."

"You want to know about Pam?" she spat, incredulous.

"It's important." I sank onto the couch, sitting with one leg tucked beneath the other. "I'm sorry it's urgent, but we need to know this."

"I haven't talked to Pam in years."

Cammie, who had poured herself a cup of coffee, stood off to the side with a satisfied smirk on her face. Her very expression made my spine prickle as if a thousand needles had been plunged into my back.

"Yes, I know, Patricia, but I need to find her."

"Why do you need to find Pam?"

I couldn't exactly confess to Patricia about my desire to help my ghost friend find out the truth about her death, now, could I?

Just as I was stumbling over an answer, Cammie sighed and crossed over. "Amateurs," she muttered. She cleared her throat and spoke in a commanding voice. "Patricia, this is deputy Forest of the…Forest Rangers over in…Blackhook?"

Cammie's eyes cut to me, silently asking if Blackhook was the actual name of a town. I shook my head. What was she talking about?

But my sister's tactic startled the sourpuss right out of Patricia. "Yes, Deputy?"

Cammie winked at me. "We've got a four-ten out for this Pam and need to know where to locate her."

"Oh." Shock filled Patricia's voice. "A four-ten, huh?"

"Ma'am, I'll be the one asking the questions."

"Right. Of course. About Pam…let me think. We lost touch a while back, but if I recall, she moved to the east side of the lake, to a smaller house. Tell you what—my nephew, Abraham, will be able to help you. He knows Willow Lake like the back of his hand. Tell him to give you directions to the general store out in East Waters. That should work."

"The general store?" Cammie's eyes gaze narrowed. "Why there?"

"You'll understand when you arrive." Patricia's voice grew faint, as if a breeze was blowing into the phone. "Is there anything else I can help you with, Deputy?"

Cammie's mouth snaked into a devilish smile. "No, that should do it." She ended the call by mashing her thumb to the screen. "Sometimes you gotta BS a BS'er."

"Not sure that applies." I took the phone. "Well, looks like we have a lead on Pam."

"Great." Cammie crossed to the bathroom. "Ugh. My mouth tastes terrible. Let me take a shower and get dressed. Then we'll call Abraham and head out." She clutched the bathroom door with her finger and pivoted her head over one shoulder. "And let's grab a bite to eat on the way. I'm starving."

After she'd disappeared into the room, I fixed my attention on Snow. "Now maybe we'll find out what happened to your husband, your family."

Her eyes cut to the floor. "Yeah. Maybe."

"Is something wrong?"

Snow's gaze darted up. "No, not at all." She hugged her arms, and her lips tipped into a smile. "This is the best day of my death. Maybe the mystery will be solved."

Snow smiled at me, but worry simmered in her eyes. Snow was already dead. What did she have to worry about?

My phone rang while Cammie sang in the shower, belting out an earsplitting rendition of Def Leppard. She'd managed to take a marathon fifteen-minute shower, convincing me that her entire goal was to drain the hot water heater of every drop of warmed water. If that wasn't her intention, then I didn't want to know what else she was doing in my bathroom.

I picked up my chirping phone and grinned like a lovesick teenager at the sight of Grim's name. "Hey, stranger," I purred, which made me choke.

Then I coughed into his ear.

"You okay?" he asked after my throat was raw.

"Yes," I squeaked. I grabbed a bottle of water from the fridge and sucked down several gulps. The cool water instantly soothed my scratchy throat. "I'm fine. Just something went down the wrong way. What's up?"

"I had a great time last night."

His velvety voice sent a shiver straddling my spine. "Me too."

"I'd like to see you tonight."

Wow, for someone intent on straying from commitment, he certainly wanted to spend some time together. I slipped my hips onto the kitchen counter and sat. "Is this part of the whole, I-don't-want-to-hide-my-heart-anymore thing?"

"And what if it is? Would that be okay?" he replied in a dark, husky voice.

"It would definitely be okay." *It would be more than okay.* "I'd like to see you."

He exhaled deeply. "Paige, Paige, Paige."

"Yes?" I was grinning and my cheeks ached from it. "Am I missing something?"

"The things you do to me."

"You don't say."

"I do say."

"Tell me more."

"I'd rather show you."

My heart slammed into my rib cage. What was going on here? I took several deep breaths to get a grip on my emotions. This was just physical, was all. Revealing your heart was different than wanting a commitment. They were two totally unrelated events.

Weren't they?

"What about tonight?" he asked.

I'd been so sucked into my thoughts that I forgot what we were talking about. "For what?"

"To see you."

"Oh, right." A nervous laugh escaped my throat. "Yes. I'd love to."

"Maybe we can swim again."

I chuckled. "Maybe so. We'll see."

We hung up after deciding that Grim would pick me up around eight. A ridiculous amount of joy rushed into my bloodstream, and I hummed as I waited for Cammie to exit the bathroom.

When she did so, in a haze of smoke and rose-scented perfume, she cocked one eye at me. "You got a date, don't ya?"

"How do you know?"

She flicked her fingers at me as her gaze licked up and down my torso. "'Cause you look all happy and stuff. Like you just had yourself a good time."

I shuddered at the innuendo. "I'm going to pretend that I didn't hear that."

"Awesome." She flung her purse over one shoulder. "Let's go get some food and hit that general store."

"Sounds like a plan."

Cammie called Abraham and got the directions. Then she wanted to eat, so we stopped at the bar and grill. Ferguson was working. I waved to him when we entered. His graying hair was combed over to one side. Fine lines ran across his forehead, making the bartender look distinguished rather than old.

Cammie rushed over to talk to him, her hands circling around his bicep. She pushed up to her tiptoes and whispered something in his ear. Ferguson chuckled and Cammie ran a long finger down his shirt collar seductively.

I studied the menu while she flirted shamelessly with Ferguson. When the server arrived at our table, I ordered French onion soup and Cammie tore herself from Ferguson long enough to order a wedge salad.

"Are you going to eat with me?" I asked. "Or flirt with your new boyfriend?"

Cammie's sneaked a look at him with hooded eyes. "I'll stay here. Just 'cause I like you," she told me in her thick Southern accent.

Cammie thought she knew Ferguson, but she didn't know what he was—a leprechaun. "So, what is it that you and Ferguson talk about? On your dates," I added, creating air quotation marks with my fingers on the last word.

She pinched her fingers across the top of her napkin before dropping it into her lap. "Well, there ain't a lot of talking. But when there is, he's funny. Cute. Makes me laugh." Her gaze latched on to him, and her eyes softened, taking on a dreamy look. "There's just something about him, I guess. We don't fight. We don't argue. We talk about big stuff—life and death. We got it all in common."

I sipped from the tea glass that the waitress had delivered. "You've got it *all* in common?"

"Yeah," she explained. "We just"—she cut the air with her hand— "get one another. I think I may marry him."

Tea spurted from my mouth, landing in huge droplets onto the table. "Oh, sorry." I mopped the mess with my napkin. "I wasn't expecting you to say that."

She rolled her eyes. "I realize that I may have a tendency to love very quickly."

"Do you think? I mean, you've been married three times."

"And all of them I'd known less than three months. Yes, I get it." She ripped the top off a straw wrapper and dunked the straw into her water. Cammie then twisted the wrapper between her fingers. "There can be more than one soulmate in the world for you," she said earnestly. "Take you and Grim."

"Oh no. We are not talking about me and Grim."

She sniffed. "I am. I'm talking about him."

"Why don't you try Newman again."

She pulled out her phone and dialed. Cammie listened for a moment and flipped the screen to me. *"The person you are trying to reach has not yet set up voice mail."*

"I ain't never going to find him."

"Oh yes, we are," I snapped.

"But back to you and Grim." I started to protest, but my sister simply drove over my words with her own. "He likes you. Seems wounded. Real deep. But he might be looking to move on if he found the right person."

"I don't know."

She sniffed. "I know. I can tell these things. How else you think I'm so good at capturing men?" Cammie tapped her temple. "I can read them, see. And from what I see about Grim, I can tell he might like you a lot."

"That shows what you know," I said triumphantly. "He's not interested in commitment. Said so himself."

"You're wrong." When my jaw dropped, she hitched a shoulder to her ear. "I'm just saying, you're wrong. Just watch. But I can also see where he'd be worried that he couldn't quite be there for you."

Now I was intrigued. My brain was screaming at me not to listen, but my heart lurched forward and so did my body. "What do you mean?"

She gazed over my shoulder as if in thought. "I don't know. I just suspect he's real big on protection. You know, that's a thing with men."

Protection? Was he worried about protecting me? From what?

Cammie had literally fallen down the psychological rabbit hole of Grim's mind, and I had plunged with her. I was about to ask her another question when a deep male voice cut into our conversation.

"Cammie," came the silky voice.

Hovering at the end of the table stood a man who was maybe in his midforties. He was short, portly and had a bird's beak of a nose. He brought his sausage fingers together with glee.

"I'm so glad that I found you," he sneered.

Cammie's lips trembled when she said, "Newman?"

CHAPTER 5

*N*ewman definitely didn't look like the mafia type, not with his portly physique, squinty eyes and eagle-like nose.

"Cammie," he purred in a voice that made me want to vomit, "I've been looking for you."

Her trembling lips stilled. My sister curled her white-knuckled fingers into her napkin. "Why ever have you been doing *that*? Last time I saw you, you were knocking boots with some floozy."

"Now, now, Cammie, we both knew what we were getting into when our relationship started." He traced a finger down the front of his shirt and made a circle where his belly button would've been. I think the move was supposed to be seductive, but instead it made bile edge up the back of my throat. "We realized early on that our love would burn bright and hot, becoming smoldering coals within weeks. That's the kind of woman you are."

Cammie's eyes were big as plates. "We did have some chemistry."

"Chemistry can only take you so far." Newman ran his finger along the top of Cammie's ear, and she shivered. "But that's not what I'm here for. You stole from me."

She shot him a frosty look. "I don't know what you're talking about."

Under the table, my toe connected with her shinbone.

"Ouch!" She bent down to rub her leg. "That hurt. Why'd you do that, Paige?"

"Because." I spoke through gritted teeth. They really were gritted. My jaw was clenched tight, and my molars were glued together in anger. "Newman is talking about something that was taken from him. Don't you want to give that back?"

She shot me a sulky look before grudgingly pouting out a reply of, "I guess so."

Newman thumbed over his shoulder. "My associates have escorted me here. Do you see them?" He pointed to a booth where a blond man wearing black leather from head to toe sat fiddling with a pocketknife. "That's Stanislav."

Stanislav glanced up and waved.

Newman placed one hand to the side of his mouth in a whisper. "He's Russian. Doesn't like to be swindled. Has a real hard time with it."

Oh no. We were dealing with the Russian mob? They were ruthless. At least, that was how every movie that dealt with the Russian mob portrayed them—as thickly accented assassins.

"And that's Pippa." Newman gestured over his other shoulder. A red-headed woman with mahogany skin stretched out her legs, revealing thigh-high patent boots that made my jaw drop. She had a lot of guts to wear boots like that out during the day. It was tempting to ask where she'd purchased them, but it didn't seem an appropriate question since clearly Newman's intention was to scare the bejesus out of us. "Pippa has a way with scents."

Cammie and I exchanged quick, confused glances. "Do you mean she smells good?" I asked.

"More than that." Newman pressed the tips of his fingers together as he grinned. His bone-chilling glee made my heart constrict. "Her scents can seduce or enrapture, kill or influence."

"She must have some stinky gas," Cammie announced.

Newman gave her a death-squint. "Do you think this is funny?"

"No, we don't." I reached across the table and gripped Cammie's arm to not so subtly hint that she needed to shut up.

Her skin was frigid. Warm air blew on us from the heating unit, but my sister's skin was awash in goose bumps. She was scared to death.

SPELL, DON'T TELL

My gaze latched on to her, and I told Newman with as much false confidence as I could muster, "We were listening."

From behind him, Pippa pulled a purple perfume bottle from her purse. A small tube ran from the lid, connecting to a deep amethyst atomizer bulb. She squeezed the bulb, and the scent spritzed over her neck. Pippa glanced over to us and parted her lips in a snakelike grin.

I shivered. That woman hadn't said one word to me, yet I didn't like her, not one bit.

"And that's Herman," Newman continued, nodding toward a small, bookwormish man in the corner booth. Herman's nose was buried deep in a book. He had shaggy brown hair, and I could just see the top of his glasses as they peeked over the cover of *The Old Man and the Sea*.

"And what can Herman do?" I asked, genuinely curious. I mean, we had a knife master, a woman with deadly scents and a bookworm. The connection between the first two was clear, but I didn't quite understand how Herman (terrible mafia name, by the way) slipped into this puzzle of assassins.

"Let's just say," Newman purred (there came that bone-chilling glee again), "that Herman's talents are *multifaceted*."

Whatever that meant. "Let's just cut to the chase, Newman. You know that my sister stole your...stuff. She has it."

His brow arched with curiosity. "*All* of it?"

"All of it," I insisted. Cammie had promised as much, and this was no time to doubt her—not when a mash-up of assassins stood knocking on our door. "You want it?"

"Well, well, well." Newman rocked back on his heels. "Indeed, I do want it."

"We can meet tonight," I told him.

"No can do tonight."

"That's the best we got." Cammie jabbed her index finger to the table. "Listen, Newman, after what you did to me, you're lucky I'm giving it back to you at all."

Fear flared down my spine as my gaze snapped to Cammie. I couldn't fight assassins. Could she? I laughed lightly and slapped my hand over Cammie's mouth, silencing her. "What my sister means is that we don't have it on us, and we have pressing business. Listen, we're not going anywhere. We can meet you tonight."

Newman's gaze shifted left and right. He didn't like what we offered, but he also didn't have a gun pointed at us, so he couldn't command that we jump just because he said so.

After a long moment his lips peeled back in a frustrated sneer. "Fine. Where should we meet?"

I told him about the spot that Snow had suggested. It was out on the lake but not too far from a gas station. We'd have privacy, but Cammie and I also wouldn't be completely isolated. If anything loud and violent occurred, the gas station attendant would hear it.

I was simply trying to keep Newman the Mafia Man as honest as I could.

We ended the conversation and Newman slinked away. It was like watching the Pillsbury Doughboy attempt to tango partnerless across a dance floor.

Not recommended for your viewing pleasure.

After he vanished out the door, his three cohorts snaked out, too. Pippa spritzed perfume on her chest as she left. Stanislav flicked his hand up and down, slinging his knife open and closed as he walked until he had disappeared out the door. And Herman, who may have possessed the most talent of all of them, kept his nose buried in the paperback and exited without once looking up.

Cammie exhaled a gusty sigh once they'd left. She dropped her face to the table and sat there a long moment.

"Are you okay?"

"Yes. No." She shot up and grabbed her hair and grimaced. "Head rush. One thing's for certain, I'll be glad when this is all over."

As I stared at the door, my stomach clenched with worry. I, too, would be relieved once the money was out of the cabin and its presence was no longer hanging over my head. But even though we'd be rid of it soon, I had a feeling that this night wouldn't go as smoothly as I hoped.

Not by a long shot.

CHAPTER 6

The general store looked like a snapshot taken from a hundred years ago—minus the sepia-drenched tones, that was.

Cammie and I had debated whether or not we should even go to the general store, since Newman's arrival had stolen the proverbial wind from our sails. But in the end I wanted to do this for Snow, to help her solve the mystery of how she'd ended up in Heronomous's book of creatures.

Also, finding Pam could help us find the book, as it was missing. Its absence created an undercurrent of tension in my stay at Willow Lake. Detailed drawings of monstrous creatures were penned in color on nearly every page, just waiting to leave their paper prisons and wreak havoc. That meant a legion of terrors could be unleashed on the town at any given time.

So, priorities and all…

The general store smelled of cinnamon sticks and fudge. Even though I'd just eaten, my stomach rumbled at the scents. A dessert case sat in the back of the store. The sign hanging above it advertised home-made fudge and chocolates.

What did you know, but my nose was right on the money.

There were all sorts of things to purchase—maps of the area, T-shirts and baseball caps with the Willow Lake logo stitched across them. I hadn't even realized the town had a logo, but it did —a crane standing tall on a log with the sun fading in the background.

There was also a section for kids—wooden toys from airplanes to rubber-band-ammunition guns. This was truly a gem of a general store, and I regretted having only just been introduced to the place.

"Howdy," came a voice from behind the counter.

A short woman with wiry gray hair appeared. She wore a blue Willow Lake baseball cap tugged to her ears and her eyeglasses swung from a beaded chain around her neck.

"What can I do you for?" she asked in a pleasant, open voice.

"Where's Pam?" Cammie insisted.

I rubbed my eyes. Would it kill my sister to learn some manners now and then? I mean, how hard was it to ask nicely?

The woman startled. "What's that?"

A nervous laugh tittered from my throat. "What my sister means is, we're looking for Pam. My landlady, Patricia, said that we'd find her here."

The woman scratched her chin and frowned. "I can't say that I know anybody by that name."

I stepped closer to the counter. The entire face of it was lined with tri-folded maps and brochures advertising local attractions and even not so local spots like Rock City, which was outside of Chattanooga. Of course, signs for the famous rocky site littered the interstates as far south as Florida, or so it seemed.

"Well," Cammie said, patting my shoulder, "you tried. You can tell Snow that."

The woman blinked. "Did you say Snow?"

"She did."

The woman ripped a yellow Post-it from a pad and scribbled something on it. She slapped the sticky side of the note down on the counter in front of me.

"Call this number." She tapped the digits that she had penned. "Ask for Pam."

My nose wrinkled in distaste. "Is this Pam's cell?"

Instead of answering directly, she said, "It's the best I can do. Ask for her. Good luck."

Cammie glanced over my shoulder at the number. "Well, it's the best we got. Let's go."

I stared at the woman for a moment longer, silently willing her to explain more about why she'd pretended not to know Pam, but all I was greeted with was silence and a stony expression. The woman turned away from us, and that ended the conversation.

I slipped the Post-it into my purse and motioned for Cammie to leave. When we reached the car, she deflated onto the seat.

"How do you think that woman kills with perfume?"

Wait. What? "Oh, you mean that Pippa lady?"

"Yep."

I thumbed on the ignition. The car roared to life, and I sat quietly while it idled, feeling the hum of it beneath me.

"I guess I don't know how she kills with smells. Maybe it's really mustard gas or something."

"Or horrible farts."

I laughed. "That's ridiculous."

"But it made you smile, didn't it?" She elbowed me. "You've been all wound up today. I know, I know. Seeing Newman did a number on me, too, what with his friends and all hanging around. I'm worried. But you cain't let a little criminal mastermind get you down. After all, you got a phone number for that Pam woman."

I gripped the gearshift and pulled the stick into gear. We slowly rumbled out of the parking lot and out onto the road. Orange and yellow fall leaves floated in the air, spinning and dancing on the asphalt.

I sighed. "The way that woman back there acted, she didn't seem confident that Pam would talk to us—at all."

"But she looked real interested when I said Snow's name."

I clicked my tongue. "She sure did."

Cammie opened her mouth and breathed fog onto the door's glass. My gaze flashed over, and I caught her drawing a C with her finger.

"What are you doing?"

"Leaving you a reminder of me." She shot me a wide grin. "Nobody ever cleans the inside of their windows, and if I die tonight, you can remember me by fogging up this spot and seeing my initial."

"You're not going to die tonight. Newman looks more capable of winning a hot dog–eating contest than he does murdering anybody."

She shivered. "It's not him that I'm worried about."

Little pricks of terror rippled over my flesh at the thought of the other three people with Newman. "Me neither."

WHEN WE REACHED THE CABIN, I threw myself into everything but thinking about the bag of money that needed to be delivered later in the evening.

Snow wasn't around, so I took my time curling my hair in preparation for my date with Grim. My plan was to drop off the cash and be home in time for the handsome hunk to pick me up. We'd have a fantastic night swimming and eating—not necessarily in that order.

Cammie flipped on the television and spent an hour laughing at *Naked and Afraid*. "We gotta apply to get on that show," she told me.

"No thanks."

When I finally finished up my hair, Snow drifted through a wall. "Hey, y'all," she called out.

"Snow!" I unplugged the curling iron and rushed from the bathroom. "We have a phone number for Pam."

Snow's bright ghostly eyes blinked in surprise. "You do?"

"Yes!" I snatched the slip of paper from my purse and wagged it in front of her. "Want to call it?"

"You know, it is so weird when you talk to folks I can't see," Cammie mumbled. "It really gets on my nerves."

"Deal with it," I snapped. "It's because of you that we might..." I couldn't finish the sentence.

"Get shot up tonight?"

"Right."

She withered but didn't argue.

I grabbed my phone and held it toward Snow. "Want me to call?"

She eyed the slip of paper with lengthy hesitation. Finally she gave her head a delicate nod. "Okay. I'm ready."

My skin buzzed with excitement as I dialed. A woman's voice picked up almost immediately. "Hello?"

Her timbre was shaky. The voice clearly belonged to an older woman, perhaps in her seventies.

I cleared my throat. "Hello, this is Paige Provey. I live in Willow Lake." *Sort of.* No need to go into specifics. "I'm currently working on a book about mysteries in the region and came across a missing woman from the nineties. Her name was Snow Murry, and her neighbor was Pam. I don't have a last name. I'm looking for her, wondering if she may have an idea what happened to Snow."

The lights on the phone died. The call had been ended. I stared at my phone in disbelief. "Did she really hang up on me?"

Cammie slid her eyes from the TV to me. "Looks like."

"Son of a gun." I shook my head in frustration and hit redial. This time my cell rang until the call was ended again. "Crap. She's ghosting us."

"She don't want to talk to you," Cammie so smartly pointed out.

"No, she doesn't." My gaze met Snow's. "I'm sorry. We'll have to try something else. Did she sound like Pam at all?"

Snow slowly bowed her shoulders in a shrug. "Can't say. Maybe? It's been a long time." She nibbled the tips of her ghostly fingers. "But why wouldn't she want to talk to you?"

I gripped my phone hard. "I don't know. But maybe good old Pam knows something about what happened to you, and I plan to find out what."

THE TIME CAME for us to leave to meet Newman. He hadn't said whether or not his ruffians would accompany him, but I had the feeling they would. Even if we couldn't see them, they would be close by, watching, waiting.

Hopefully they wouldn't interrupt our escape. Cammie and I had conjured a plan, one we intended to stick to.

I drove with white-knuckled fingers along the bends and twists in the road that hugged the lake. The sun had just set. The moon was high, and stars blanketed the sky above us. The moonlight scattered onto the crystalline lake waters, dancing off the surface like jewels.

"Okay. Let's go over it again. What are you going to do?"

Cammie answered in a bored voice. "We've already gone over this, like, three times."

"I want it glued into your memory."

She exhaled, deflating onto the seat. "Fine. I hand over the bag and we step away, not turning our backs to him. If he pulls a gun, I close my eyes." She frowned. "I don't get why I close my eyes."

"Because I'll already have your gun on him," I lied. "If I have to shoot, the sparks will be bright at night. We need to be able to run."

But my plan was different. To keep Newman from following us or sending his lackeys sniffing at my door, I had to scare him and good. If pudgy boy even hinted that he intended to stalk us, I would hit him with magic. I'd been working it in my belly all afternoon, making sure it was stoked like a blacksmith's forge, blazing and ready to use.

"Then we leave," Cammie said.

I nodded. "Then we leave. That's it. Got it?"

"I'd have to be a birdbrain not to get it." She pointed to a fork in the road. "This is it, right?"

"This is it," I murmured, my stomach tight with worry.

The car jostled as we turned off the asphalt at the gas station. The business lights shone brightly, and a couple of cars were parked out front. I liked the look of that. It offered a pinch of comfort in a nerve-fraying situation.

We made our way slowly down the gravel path. Potholes lined one side of the road, and I straddled the middle to keep from hitting them. Up about two hundred yards was a turnoff to the left onto a patch of grass half-covered by a row of pines.

We arrived and I made a three-point turn, aiming the nose of the car toward the entrance in case we had to make a hasty escape.

My breath came in shallow snatches of air, and I forced myself to take several deep gulps to steady myself.

"Let's get out," I told her.

We did so. Cammie clutched the bag to her side. The black nylon bulged, and even though it was zipped tight, the scent of thousands of dollars wafted through the nooks and crannies and trickled up my nostrils.

Two headlights beamed in front of us, bouncing down the road. "He's here."

We huddled beside one another, our shoulders touching, offering a smidgen of comfort. Newman pulled up into the jetty and parked off from us, on the other side of the strip of grass. He drove an old Lincoln Continental, nondescript enough to be ignored but gangster enough to be, well, gangster.

Newman flung open the door and after several seconds of huffing and puffing, he finally scooted out of the seat.

"Ladies," he cooed. "So glad you could join us."

"Us?" My gaze flicked from tree to tree. "Are others here?"

"Oh yes, just to make sure that you don't try any funny business."

"*Us?*" My jaw dropped. "All we want is to get rid of this bag."

He snickered, his jowls quivering. "If that was true, you would've contacted me."

"Your voice mail ain't set up," Cammie informed him.

"Oh yes. I've been busy," he replied, quickly covering for his ineptitude. "Now. The money."

Before we could move, the three weirdo associates slinked from the tree line. Stanislav fidgeted with his knife. Pippa lifted a glittery crystal vial, apparently threatening us with death by perfume, and Herman glided onto the grass, nose-deep in a new book. Couldn't read the title.

I nodded to Cammie, and she stalked forward and thrust the bag into Newman's thick arms, but he didn't grab hold. "There. You can have your stupid money. I never wanted it to begin with. You were the worst tussle I've ever had, anyway."

"Open it," Newman told her.

Cammie scoffed, super annoyed. She shook her head, mumbling something about this being the last time she ever did anything for Newman. Then she dumped the duffel on the ground and with a flourish of her hand, unzipped the bag.

"There? You see? It's all there, every last dollar. If you want to count it in front of us, feel free."

"That won't be necessary."

He nodded to his three companions, and they slinked back into the pines, disappearing into the dark shadows that cloaked the trees.

Once they were gone, Newman smiled brightly. "I'll just be taking my money and going. See you around, Cammie." His gaze roamed over her body, his eyes shining with brutal distaste. "We probably won't see one another ever again, and even then, it'll be too soon. Ta-ta!"

He turned on his heel and waddled to his car. It took a moment for the insult to sink into Cammie. When it did, she crossed her arms with a huff. "That jerk."

I squeezed her shoulder. "He's a jerk, but it's done. The money is his and you don't have to worry about being killed over it now. So I'd say, count your blessings."

"I guess so," she muttered.

Newman bumbled into his seat and shut the door. He gave us one last wave and cranked the engine. I heard the sound of the transmission kicking in as he shifted into reverse.

Then the car exploded.

CHAPTER 7

I fell flat on my butt and watched as fire poured from the windows. The undercarriage buckled as the force of the explosion lifted the vehicle into the air and then gravity slammed it back down.

I grabbed Cammie. She grabbed me.

"Oh crap," she mumbled.

"Oh crap is right."

Fear ignited down my spine, and I worried for a moment that one of the three assassins would slink back from the trees and attack us, thinking that we had stowed a bomb in the bag, but none of them appeared.

At least, not yet.

"We should leave," Cammie insisted.

"Leave a crime scene?"

Panic filled her eyes. "They'll want to know why we were here, and we'll have to tell them about the money. Look!"

Blazing dollar bills rained down on the vehicle, having been thrown into the sky when it exploded. "It's not going to be a secret," I told her.

"But if we stay, then we'll look guilty. We'll look like we did something," she insisted.

"*You* did do something. You took the money."

"Yes, but only accidentally-on-purpose."

I shook my head. Red and orange light flickered over Cammie's tortured expression. She didn't want to be found anywhere near Newman. I understood that. But it would be worse for us if the police tracked us down after the fact. They would question us harder, and if Grim discovered that I may have been involved with a bombing or whatever had happened here, then our relationship would go up in flames—no pun intended.

"If you want to go, go," I told my sister. "But I'm calling the police." A siren blared in the distance. "Well, maybe I don't have to call after all. They're probably on their way."

"I'll stay," she muttered grudgingly.

The fire truck and police arrived almost at the same time. The firemen sprayed the sedan with white powder, and within a few minutes the fire was gone, and the vehicle was smoking. Newman's charred carcass sat slumped in the driver's seat.

I hadn't known him, and what I'd seen I hadn't liked, but I took no joy in witnessing his roasted body behind the steering wheel.

Officer Cowan was on duty, it turned out. He moseyed in with a pencil behind his ear and a pad in his hand. He took one look at the car and then one look at me and Cammie and started asking questions.

We came clean about everything. A couple of times I had to elbow Cammie to get her to fess up, but she was mostly forthcoming.

"And then he put the vehicle in reverse, and it exploded," I told the officer.

He scratched his head. Cowan looked like a grown-up elf. He wasn't, though. But his ears were a tiny bit pointed at the tips instead of smoothly rounded off and his chin was angled. It was, I'd decided, a complete fluke that he'd wound up looking like he belonged in a Christmas movie. Cowan knew about the hidden magic in Willow Lake, but he himself wasn't blessed with having been born magical.

He'd once hinted that he may have come from werewolves, but if that was the case, the wolf gene had somehow skipped him—if that was possible. Not sure doggy DNA worked that way.

But anyhow, back to the interrogation. The deputy shook his head. "So you handed him the dirty money."

"Drug cash," Cammie told him. "More than likely."

42

"Got it, drugs." He penned that into his book. "And when Newman was going to leave, his car exploded."

"That's it." She brushed her hands together like she was dusting that man from her life. "End of story. Nothing more to tell."

"And do you know who could've done this? Who would've wanted to kill Newman?"

Cammie scoffed. "Well me, if I could've kept the money scot-free."

I felt my head slowly turn in Cammie's direction. My eyes opened wide, and I stared at her, wanting to bore a hole smack in her forehead.

She recognized my expression of doom and scrambled to add, "But we didn't do it. Not at all. I don't know who did. But he did have some friends."

"Friends?" Cowan leaned forward. "Tell me all about them."

While Cammie was chatting away with Cowan, I spotted Grim's motorcycle roaring down the road. What was he doing here?

Great. I didn't want him to see me at a crime scene. We had a date tonight. A date that I might have to cancel because there was no telling how long Cowan's interrogation would last. But I was holding out hope that I'd still be able to swing a little pool time.

Grim parked his bike. I scanned the area, praying to spot a tree that I could duck behind for the next thirty minutes or however long he stayed.

I'd just spotted a frilly spruce when a voice murmured in my ear, "Was this your plan for our date tonight? To wind up tangled in a murder?"

I whirled around and there stood Grim. With my brilliant idea to blend in with the foliage ruined, I had no choice but to engage him in conversation.

I laughed lightly in a pathetic attempt to cover my discomfort of him finding me connected with all this Newman mess. *Way to go, Cammie! Thanks for dragging me into your circus of monkeys.*

"Oh, this?" I replied, eyes blinking in a flirty way. "I was hoping you'd find this appealing."

"Is there something in your eye?"

I stopped blinking. "No. Well, there was. But it's gone."

"Huh." Grim folded his arms. "I got a call about an explosion, and I find you here. You doing research?"

"Um no." Here came the fun part. "I was here when it happened."

Worry flashed in his jewel-toned eyes. "Are you okay?"

Oh my goodness, this must've been some deep infatuation sizzling between us because for Grim to ask if I was okay instead of why I happened to be present at the scene of a crime made my heart like him a little bit more.

His razor-sharp jawline and glittering eyes helped with that, too. And so did his Roman statue–like body. Just letting my gaze trace down his torso set my body humming with feelings that may be too racy to describe here.

But back to Grim's concern (and how it was so charming) for my well-being.

I cringed. "Yeah. It's a whole story. I'll tell you later."

He nodded hard. "Let me check in with Cowan."

Cowan said something to Cammie when Grim approached, and she spotted me and came over. "Where'd you run off to?" she asked in an accusing voice.

"For your information, I was trying to figure out how to *not* be spotted by Grim, who is here."

She flicked away my concern with her hand. "Men love to be knights in shining armor. It's their thing. He finds out you almost went boom along with the car and he'll be sweeping you off your feet and laying you down in his bed quicker than you can say, 'pancakes.'"

"Pancakes," I teased. "Oh, look. He's still talking to Cowan."

She scowled. "You know what I mean."

"I do." Steering the conversation away from Grim, I asked, "What did Cowan say?"

"Not much. I told him about the three freaks that were tagging along with Newman."

I scoffed. "Good luck finding them. I'm sure as soon as the explosion occurred, they were gone. Outta here. Never to be seen again."

"Probably," she mused. "But why would someone have wanted to kill Newman?"

I shrugged, not caring. "Who knows? The sort of people he ran with weren't exactly the kind to kiss and tell."

"But he had the money," she persisted. "It was in his hands. Heck, he was about to be gone. Now all the cash is gone."

I swore Cammie whimpered a little bit on that last line. "Maybe it was a revenge killing for something else. What do people murder over? Money, love. What else?"

She considered that with her head cocked. "They also murder to cover their tracks. What if Newman knew something that he wasn't supposed to? What if he stumbled into something that was too big for him and he was murdered to stay quiet?"

I patted her shoulder. "Okay, Columbo. You go figure it out. I'm done. We gave Newman the money. End of story. As far as I'm concerned, our part with this is over. I'm ready to get back to my life, and you should be, too. Now you don't have to stay with me anymore, hiding out in fear for your life. You can go back and live it. I'm sure Newman told whoever his boss is that he was meeting you to get the money. Of course, he'll also find out that Newman was killed after he got it back."

A prickle of unease tingled my spine. My mind kept drifting. What if Newman's boss discovered the murder and he or she thought that Cammie was responsible? Just as worry made my heart contract with fear, I realized that was preposterous. Why would Cammie deliver the goods and then destroy them? It made no sense. Anyone with half a brain would see that was a silly possibility.

I exhaled a deep sigh. Cammie should be off the hook with the mob. After all, she'd done her job by delivering the cash.

Grim parted ways with Cowan, and he crossed to the car, walking around it. Lamps had been set up at the perimeter. They cast a bright white light on the expanse of grass that jutted out into the lake. Grim strode with purpose, bending to study something.

Intrigued, I walked over to him. A lot of the grass was charred around the vehicle, so I wondered what it was that he could've been studying.

"Any clues there?" I asked.

His gaze cut to me, sending a shiver straight to my bones. "I know what you were doing here."

Oh, that. Right. "Cammie made a mistake," I explained, trying to make light of the situation. "She got involved with Newman, that guy." I pointed to the smoking corpse that still sat in the vehicle. "She stole

45

some money from him, and I didn't know about it until recently—like yesterday."

He ran his fingers along the charred grass. "Were you going to tell me?"

Why was I suddenly feeling on the defense? "Burden you with my problems? No, I wasn't. Is that an issue?"

"It's not if you're not *with* someone," he said coldly.

His words hit me like a slap. "What's that supposed to mean?" And why were we having an argument in the middle of a crime scene? We were supposed to be on a date in—I checked my watch—thirty minutes.

He closed his eyes and blew out a breath. "It's nothing. Sorry. I'm just surprised by it all."

"Join the club." I studied him, my gaze skimming over his clenched jaw. "If you're worried that I'm going to bring death to your door, you don't have to be. This was my only brush with the wrong type of people, and it wouldn't have happened if it hadn't been for my sister."

Grim's expression darkened. "It's not you I'm worried will bring death."

Okay, cryptic much? "Um. Well…" I wasn't sure what was happening. Grim's demeanor had flipped one-eighty. I hated to ask if we were still going on our date, but I really needed to know, because if my proximity to an exploding car dampened the chemistry between us, I wanted to know now—before I fell any more head over heels for him.

He rose and brushed his hands on his thighs. "I'll only be a moment and then we can leave. But I understand if you don't want to go out and instead want to be with your sister. Family is important."

That dark look blazed across his face again. The mystery surrounding Grim intrigued me. I'd be lying if I said the writer part of me wasn't fascinated by him. The little I knew, I liked. But Grim wasn't the sort to start talking and let all his secrets spill from his tongue. No, he only relayed bits and pieces of information at a time.

I wanted to know more, I realized. I wanted to know everything about him. I wanted to feast on every detail he had to share.

He waited for my response, so I told him, "I'll take Cammie home and make sure she's okay. Then we can decide what to do."

Grim escorted me back to Cowan. As we crossed the grass, his hand rested on my lower back. Warmth leaked from his palm, sinking into my skin. It was the most natural thing to be this way with him, to feel his presence so closely. He was a mystery, but at the same time, when our gazes locked, I felt like I'd known Grim all my life, that we were connected on a level that I'd never known could exist with someone else.

It certainly hadn't been that way with Walter. Or perhaps it was in the beginning, but that had quickly faded.

Cowan shifted his focus from Cammie to Grim. "Find anything?"

Grim nodded. "I sure did."

The deputy scratched his head. "Do you know what it means?"

"Maybe. Come take a look."

CHAPTER 8

*G*rim's revelation nearly knocked me on my rump. He'd found something? While we'd been chatting?

I was slightly offended that he hadn't told me, but seeing as how I wasn't law enforcement, I couldn't be too ticked, now could I?

"Whatcha got?" Cowan asked.

"Yeah." Cammie peered around Cowan's arm at Grim. "What've you got?"

Cowan suddenly seemed to realize that civilians were tagging along. He turned to Cammie and me, hands up. "Ladies, I'm afraid that this is official police business. Can't have y'all here."

"Crap," Cammie muttered. "Knew I shoulda kept my mouth shut."

"I'll take her home," I said to the men.

Grim's gaze fluttered over me once before he focused back on Cowan. I steered Cammie away as the men began to speak.

"Wonder what they could've found?" she said, glancing over her shoulder.

I dragged her toward the car. "Whatever it is, I'm sure it's none of our business."

"But how could they find anything? Maybe it was part of the bomb that killed Newman. I hate to speak ill of the dead—"

"But you're going to anyway."

"He was a sorry person. You cain't treat people the way that he treated me and not get your just deserts in the end."

I supposed she was right in a grotesquely honest way. "Yeah. I'm sorry about what happened."

"Long as I'm alive, I'm fine." Cammie flung open the car door and slumped inside. "Let's get going. I'm exhausted. You still having a date with Mr. Hunky?"

I slid into the car and fastened my belt. "I don't know. Seems weird to have a date when we just witnessed a man die."

"Nonsense." Cammie patted my shoulder reassuringly. "Builds character."

As I steered the car onto the gravel, I wasn't so sure that I wanted to build the sort of character within myself that Cammie was referring to.

WHEN GRIM PICKED me up at eight o'clock, the first thing I said was, "We can cancel if you want."

His eyes searched me. "I don't, unless you do."

"I don't."

He took my hand and led me to his car. Yes, he'd apparently gone home, dropped off the motorcycle and returned in his sporty new vehicle.

We drove in silence along the lake. I couldn't help but be reminded of the drive I'd made only a short while ago. A shudder wound around my spine.

Silence bled throughout the cabin, and I fixed my attention on the moonlight pouring over the trees and onto the lake to distract myself.

The landscape lit up as if it had been forged in silver. Willow Lake was truly beautiful, a mesmerizing town.

Grim came to a stop outside a restaurant. "I think this is safe."

"Safe?" I said, my mouth drying.

"I'll explain when we're seated."

We sat at an open-air picnic table. There were several stationed outside of the restaurant. It looked like an old filling station, one with a shop, had been converted into a store. Steel-framed glass garage doors were pushed open, and a man with slicked-back ebony hair trekked outside holding two red food baskets lined with paper. Inside sat tacos spilling with meat and vegetables.

I caught a whiff as he passed me—the rich aromas of cumin and lime trailed behind him. My stomach rumbled loudly. I pressed a hand to it, hoping no one had heard.

As I glanced around, I realized where we were. "Is this the east side of town?"

Grim's gaze scoured the menu. "It is. Why?"

"I was here earlier today. I'm looking for someone."

Grim thumbed to the man. "His name's Al. Knows everybody. He may be able to help you."

Al deposited the food and approached us. He patted Grim's shoulder and grinned so happily that his smile was contagious. "Grim, my friend. Good to see you. It's been a while."

"Sorry that I haven't made my way here earlier."

Al shook his head. "No worries. But I suspect that you were present after that horrible tragedy that happened tonight." His brows pinched together with worry. "Anything I need to be concerned about?"

"Don't know yet, but I doubt it. From the looks of the accident, it appears this was targeted to one person."

Al exhaled. "Good to know." His gaze shifted to me, and for the first time Al acknowledged my presence. "And you've brought a lady friend, I see. Welcome to Al's. We make the best tacos in all of Willow Lake."

"They smell heavenly."

"And taste even better," he said with a wink. "Would you like to peruse the menu."

"I don't think so. I'll have your specialty."

"Ah!" His eyes danced with delight. "That's pork belly."

"I'll try it."

He smiled contentedly. "And for you, Grim? The usual?"

"No." Grim tapped the menu onto the table. "I'll have the same. And I'll also have a beer."

"Me too," I chirped.

Al took the menu and folded into a half bow. "Coming right up."

He quickly returned with our food and drinks. The pork belly was seasoned to perfection, and it was fried, giving it a crispy edge. The sharp saltiness of it mixed with the tomatoes and vegetables made my taste buds jump with happiness.

"This is amazing," I said with a moan. "Wish I'd known about this place before."

"I can't reveal all my secrets on the first date," Grim joked.

I folded my hands together. "Why'd you say that you thought this place was safe."

"Because that's what I meant." He took a pull from his beer, and when he set it down, his energy shifted. His gaze roved our surroundings, his eyes narrowing as if he was searching, waiting for a beast to lunge at us from the darkness. "This place is safe."

"Does this have to do with what you showed Cowan?"

"Yes."

When he didn't offer any more details, I prodded him. "Are you going to tell me about it?"

He wiped his mouth with a napkin. "I'm sorry for being testy earlier. You have to understand. My job is a hunter. I hunt monsters. I make sure creatures don't jump out of closets."

"How did you wind up even doing this for a living?"

His jaw twitched. "It's a long story."

"I like finding things out about you."

From under the table, his fingers grazed my knee. A jolt of desire darted to my toes. "And I like learning about you, too."

"So tell me how you got into this business."

His gaze sharpened as if he thought that by staring at me, I'd back down. Little did he know, but I had the patience of an elephant.

Grim sighed and nodded. "I come from a normal magical family. My mom stayed at home while my father did what I do."

My brows shot to peaks. "He hunted as well?"

"He did."

I frowned. "This is an entire world that I never even knew existed. I feel cheated, in a way. Like, I could have known about all of this years ago."

He quirked a brow. "And what would you have done with it? Knowing that there's a book filled with real monsters, knowing that there's a blood ice cream for vampires, that there's a werewolf grocery store. What would that have done for you?"

The amber ring in his eyes blazed like fire. His gaze felt like a blow-torch, the heat a furnace blasting on my face. My eyes cut away, and I replied, "I would have known you, maybe."

Grim dropped what was left of his taco onto the basket and pushed it forward. "That would have been the one positive, because even though magic is useful, it helps people, the monsters that come with it are dangerous—and I don't just mean to people."

Other diners sat at tables sprinkled around us, but in this moment I forgot about them. They melted into the background, and it was just Grim and me sitting under a canopy of stars, staring into one another's eyes.

Shivers danced up my spine as he spoke, and I instinctively knew that this story was not going to end well.

"What happened then?" I gently prodded.

My hands rested on the table. I wasn't eating. Witnessing him reveal intimate details of his life intrigued me. One crunch of lettuce between my teeth and I could miss an important detail.

Grim traced a line over my forearm. When he reached my palm, he turned it over and studied my hand. For a brief moment I worried that he would shut down, but to my relief he continued.

"My father was always very careful about hunting. When he was on the trail of a beast, he never came home. It was to ensure our safety. Some creatures have more intelligence than others, though, as you might expect." His gaze flashed up to me, and his eyes met mine. In the darkness they looked like pools of ink that shimmered under the moonlight. "There were precautions of course, too. The house was charmed and layered with protection shields to keep us safe. They worked until they didn't."

A ribbon of worry tightened in my chest. I had a feeling that I knew what would come next, but I didn't want to interrupt him.

"Near our house—and we lived in a forest with a stream running behind it—there was a meadow of wildflowers. It was a fairy tale of an existence that we had back then. My mother schooled my sister and me during the day. Oh, we went to town and had friends, but we were a close, close family. But there was a meadow, and in that meadow I met a small man. That's what I thought it was. We became friends. He told me stories that made me laugh, but he said that I was never to tell anyone about him, for he and I were secret friends."

I could just imagine a young Grim with a bright smile and big, kind eyes playing with this man.

"You have to understand," he said earnestly, "there was nothing malicious in him. My father had told us that monsters were evil, that the darkness inside of them was too much to contain; that was why most of them were ugly. They couldn't hide their hideous nature from the world because it was too great. That was what I grew up knowing. I wish..." He pulled his hand from mine and curled it into a fist. "I wish that I'd known then that not all monsters are ugly. This was the first that I would ever meet of that type. The second"—darkness flashed in his eyes— "well, you know that story."

I very much did. In that tale, Grim fell in love with a woman who ate people—literally. He'd fallen for a monster, and she'd almost killed him.

Talk about fatal beauty.

"We became friends, this man and me. One day my father came home from a successful expedition. He'd taught me a little bit here and there about how to hunt. I was nine at the time and just learning these things, so I still didn't know much. But our world was safe. The meadow and house, the stream—my parents believed that whatever spells they had placed on these areas, they would protect us from harm. And they had, up until that point."

He sighed heavily and sat back, dragging his fingers along the table as he did so. Grim stopped for a moment and I didn't know if he would continue, but I waited. He raked his fingers down his face and began again.

"But the man, he tricked me. Told me that my parents were in danger and that he could help them. So I brought him to our home. I led him right to our door. I opened it to find my father and mother in the kitchen. My father took one look at the man and lifted his hand to fight, but it was too late. The old man was already changing, turning into a creature with ropes for arms and legs. It killed my father almost instantly."

My heart sliced in two. A great wave of pain rocked my body. Tears pricked my own eyes at his pain. "And your mother?" I ventured.

Grim shook his head. "She went next."

CHAPTER 9

"The creature killed her as swiftly as he did my father. All I could do was stare at the mess, stare at their lifeless bodies. Then it hit me what had happened. That I'd been betrayed, used, deceived. My magic hadn't come in yet, but I grabbed the only weapon I could find—a baseball bat, and I was determined to harm the little man who'd pretended to be my friend."

A cold wind slid through the night, and I shivered, hugging my arms. It brought with it the faint smell of woodsmoke. Someone somewhere had lit a fire in their chimney. The familiar smell offered little comfort right now, however.

"I attacked him," Grim confessed. "But I was too young to have harmed the monster. He looked at me and laughed, told me that I'd trusted the wrong person, that I'd made the wrong friend. Then he turned and left, leaving me alone. My sister had been down at the stream at the time. When she returned and saw the mess, she screamed and screamed. Her wails were so loud and the emotional distress so great that her magic was ignited, and her screams called our family to us, and they saw what had happened."

He slid back onto his seat and exhaled. "And that's the story. That's the end of it. My aunt and uncle raised us from there. He was also a hunter, and he taught me everything that I know."

"I'm so, so sorry," I told him. The words seemed hollow, offering little consolation to a man who'd experienced such horrors as a child. But even I knew there was little I could say that he hadn't heard before. "You were only a child. But you know that."

"I trusted the wrong person," he said coldly. "Doing so cost my parents their lives. My sister has never forgiven me."

I frowned, wondering how she could hurt Grim more when he clearly still suffered from this wound. "I can understand her blaming you when you were younger, but as you grew up that didn't change?"

"No." He said it so frostily I didn't think that he'd continue, but he did. "She said that I should have known the man was evil. But she never met him, never saw him. My uncle told me later what the creature was —a darkling."

I cocked a brow. "A what?"

"Darkling. They're people who are overcome with an evil spirit. They become seeped in despair and sadness. That evil overtakes their bodies like a virus, transforming them into something evil. That particular creature had encountered my father before. They had fought and the creature had lost an arm. It didn't get over that. All it wanted was revenge. So it tracked down my father, but the protective shields stopped it from being able to enter or even come close to our home. Then it saw me. The creature knew it would have to earn my trust, so it changed its appearance and worked its way into my heart until it was confident that I would never believe it capable of harm. Well, it was right."

"And did you ever find it again?"

"Not me. My uncle and other family members did. They tracked it down and destroyed it."

"I'm sure you didn't want to see that."

Grim glanced up at me in surprise. "My family made me identify it. I had to tell them that this was the creature who had killed my father and mother. Then they destroyed it with magic."

My mouth dried. "You watched?"

"There was no comfort in witnessing his demise, if that's what you're asking. There was also nothing gruesome about it. I was older at this point—fifteen. At that age I was learning to be a hunter. I'd already traveled with my uncle to track monsters that were harming towns, cities." He leaned forward with such intensity that sparks of magic flared off his golden skin. "You'd be surprised where creatures like to hide. Cities are the obvious choice because they're so large it's easy for them to slink into the shadows and disappear. But small towns offer a nice place to retire to. Monsters that can pass for us, humans, who want to forget about their pasts, like to slip into the cracks of places like Willow Lake, because no one would ever suspect that they exist, that they're here, among us."

His words caught in my throat. Never, not once, did I ever think of monsters as people. I thought of them as obvious monstrosities. But their real talents lay in their ability to camouflage themselves as one of us. I shuddered.

"And your sister? Did she ever forgive you?"

"No," he told me in voice cold as chips of ice. "Never. I wish that I could say differently, but that would be lying. We rarely talk."

"Does she hunt monsters, too?"

He nodded. "She does, but she has the uncanny ability of making sure that we never cross paths."

I wouldn't pretend to understand his sister's wounds. Losing both parents at such a young age changed the course of both Grim's and his sister's lives.

My heart split in two for his obvious pain. He kept so much to himself. While I studied him, staring at his beautiful hard face, watching as the wind blew several strands of his hair into his eyes, I realized that my heart had not only softened to him, but that it was filling with love for him. I felt myself falling into him. It had been so long since I'd felt anything like this that it took me a moment to recognize it.

But there was no mistaking what it was—the first stirrings of love in my heart.

"What is it?" he asked.

I must've had a stupid-looking expression on my face from feeling all that mushy love stuff. I fluffed the bottom of my hair and shook my head.

"Nothing. I was just thinking about your sister is all."

"You looked very happy to be thinking about her."

Busted! My fingers suddenly became quite interesting. My gaze dropped to them. "It was nothing. I'm just sorry this happened to you."

When my gaze lifted, Grim's eyes met mine and I was sucked into them. They held so much power that gazing into them felt like a punch to the throat. The weight of the emotion leaking from him made my heart flutter in my neck.

But he couldn't have been feeling what I was, right? It was too much to ask for. I'd been with Walter so long that I didn't know what love was anymore. I hadn't experienced it, not truly, in, goodness, twenty years.

When I was growing up, I always liked boys who never returned my feelings. I got used to things being one-sided. Yes, Grim confessed that he was tired of hiding his heart, but that didn't mean he would hand it to me on a silver platter to do with as I pleased.

His wounds ran deep. And in my experience, men who suffered from deep wounds didn't let their hearts get torched again.

"How was everything?"

Al had appeared out of nowhere to gather our empty food baskets.

I took the opportunity to lean back in the seat and pin my focus on anyone but Grim. "It was great," I said. "Best tacos I've had in ages."

He gave a little bow. "Thank you. Ever since I was a teenager, I'd wanted to open a taco restaurant and here we are."

With him at the table, I had to ask about Pam. "I'm not from the area, but I'm looking for someone who lives around here."

He quirked a dark brow. "Perhaps I know them. A lot of people eat here. A *lot*."

"With such good food, who could blame them?" He smiled at that, and I said, "Her name's Pam. Sorry, I don't have a last name. She would be perhaps, in her sixties or so. A friend of mine is searching for her."

His expression shut down. Al's eyes narrowed and the lines on his forehead deepened to the desperately-in-need-of-Botox level.

The open smile that had brushed his lips became a hard line. "I don't know what you're talking about."

"It's a who, not a what."

He shrugged as if thinking, *details, details.* "But if I were you"—the warning in his voice sent a chill wrapping down my spine—"I would stay far, far away from anyone named Pam. That's even if I knew who you were talking about."

My mouth fell in surprise. What had I done to elicit such a frigid response? Al had gone from being open and nice to his chin being set hard and his shoulders tight with tension.

Al turned to Grim. "It was nice seeing you again, Grim. Come back anytime."

He did not say that to me, I noticed. Grim met my gaze as soon as Al was out of earshot. "I haven't seen him like that before."

"Well, he was just then."

He covered his hand with mine, and little sparks of heat fluttered on my skin. "Don't worry about it. Tell you what—I'll see what I can dig up about this Pam."

I had to stop myself from smiling. He would do that for me? "Isn't this a little below your pay grade? Pam isn't exactly a monster."

He arched a perfectly delicious brow. "How do you know?"

"Well," I hesitated, "I suppose that I don't."

He rose and pulled me up. We stood there a moment, staring at one another while the cool wind wrapped itself around my legs. Grim was all heat, his body practically a furnace. I relished the warmth coming off him as he whispered in my ear, his lips caressing my skin, "Ready to go?"

A knot lumped up in my throat. "Yes," I whispered.

He led me to his car, and we rode in silence for a few minutes. I didn't know where we were going, and I didn't care.

But it was while I watched blurred trees and streaming lights whiz by that I remembered what he'd said earlier. "What did you mean when you told me that you thought the taco restaurant was safe? What was that all about?"

He leaned his head back in the seat. "What I meant was exactly that, it was safe."

"From what?" He shifted and I sensed that what I'd asked made him uncomfortable. "Grim, is there something you're not telling me?"

"No, there's just something I haven't said yet."

"That's the same thing."

His eyes cut to me, and his lips curled in a smirk. "I was hoping to investigate this before you remembered what I'd said."

"You just said it tonight."

"I know." He sighed. "Come on. I'll show you."

"Show me what?"

"What it is that I thought we'd be safe from back there."

Houses came into sight. The spaces between them narrowed, and I realized we were getting closer to downtown. "Where are we going?"

"My house."

"What do you have in your house that you can show me?"

He turned to look at me full-on, and the expression in his eyes was so chilling that my breath caught. "There's a lot that I can show you. There are monsters of all kinds hidden there. And if you want to learn how to protect yourself from them, that's the best place to start."

I swallowed the lump that had formed in my throat. Now I was protecting myself from monsters? What sort of secret did Grim have?

As the car picked up speed again and the houses became a blur, I realized that I didn't know a thing about the evils that lay in Willow Lake.

But I was about to find out.

CHAPTER 10

Grim's house was as it always was—warm and cozy with Savage greeting us upon entering. For a man's house, it wasn't sparsely furnished with a black leather couch and TV screen so large that it filled an entire wall.

His couches were *brown* leather, but there were crocheted throw blankets tossed on them, and the TV was a modest size, not so large that you needed to watch it while sitting one county over.

Savage greeted me by placing his nose in my palm. I ran my hand over the silky fur on his head, and satisfied, he padded off to his doggy bed.

Grim led me past his greenhouse, and I said to him, "Didn't you tell me that your mother had built that?"

He stopped and turned around. His eyes scanned the door leading to the space. "She did. It was at our old house. I had it moved here."

My heart softened even more to him. This was a man who'd deeply loved his family. I mean, who moves part of their house to his new one? Not some coldhearted monster hunter, but a deep-thinking man.

We stopped in his kitchen. Grim kicked a rug to one side with his foot, revealing a cellar door cut into the floorboards.

He lifted a metal ring that lay flush with the floor and pulled. The hinges were silent as the wood lifted. That could only mean one thing.

"You come down here a lot."

Grim nodded. "You'll see why in a moment."

He disappeared down the wooden stairs. I peered over the edge, but I couldn't see anything but inky darkness. A light flipped on, illuminating the oak steps.

Grim's handsome face appeared, and his hand reached for me. "Come on. It doesn't bite."

"You *say* that," I murmured.

He chuckled and for the first time that evening, a spark of happiness alighted on his face. "Paige, there's nothing down here that'll bite you. Cut you, maybe. But only if you get too close."

I rolled my eyes. "That does not fill me with confidence."

"Does it help that this is my space?"

"Maybe. But I'm beginning to wonder what other surprises you have in store for me. You already have a magical greenhouse. What's next?"

"Come down and you'll see."

"Fine." I exhaled with an annoyed huff and headed down the steps.

The inside of the cavern was bigger than I thought. The floor was cut deeply into the ground, and the ceiling was higher than I expected it to be.

Prickles of magic danced over my skin. "This place is charmed, isn't it?"

"Now what would make you say that?" he teased.

"Everything about it." I paused a moment to really take it all in. My gaze roved over the cellar, which wasn't a cellar at all. Okay, it was technically as it was underground, but the walls and the floor were finished off. This was another room, albeit one that existed beneath the earth's crust.

The walls were lined with earth-toned stacked stone. The floor was covered with the same unfinished stone. It wasn't smooth. There were rises and falls in each rock, but it worked. I liked it.

But it was what lined the walls that stole my breath.

Weapons of every shape and size were secured to the perimeter. There must've been at least ten different hunting bows, each one loaded with an arrow and ready to shoot. Beside the bows were several old-fashioned maces, the spikes on the metal balls sharpened to steely points. There were also rifles and handguns, leather whips and swords

—short swords and large, heavy broadswords, the type that it took two hands to hold and swing.

Grim watched me with curiosity. My mouth opened and shut again. I wasn't sure what to say. But when I finally found my voice, I squeaked out, "This...this is an armory."

"Right. Which is why I never show a girl on the first date. She might think I'm a serial killer."

"It is a fair assumption."

He chuckled and took my hand. His fingers left flames burning on my skin. Not literally.

"This," he said proudly, "is from several lifetimes of family collecting these pieces. Much of it I inherited from my father's collection of weapons. But a lot I gathered on my own."

"So this is what makes you feel safe?"

He shook his head. "No. This doesn't. It helps, but so does my magic. There are creatures that are immune to magic, so that's where these come in handy. But that isn't what I wanted to show you."

"There's more?" I knew that I sounded dumbfounded. But I had the right to sound that way because I was. "What else could you possibly be hiding."

"Not hiding," he corrected.

In the very back of the room (why are things always tucked in a corner?) sat an artist's workbench. Hanging above it were pictures painted in watercolor. If I'd been expecting sunsets kissed with the orange glow of the sun and mountain ranges dusted with snow, then I would've been sorely disappointed.

These watercolors portrayed monsters. Some were hideous, grotesque creatures with horns and multiple eyes. They were the things of nightmares. They were beautifully painted, but I knew that only evil lurked inside the skins of these beasts.

And still more mysteries about Grim were revealed. Every time we were together, I peeled back another layer of his personality.

All of it made me want him more.

Under the lights, the steel tips of the arrows glinted and the sharp points on the maces sparkled. But while I could easily understand their destructive beauty, it was the paintings that drew me—grotesque creatures covered in eyes, long arms blanketed with roping veins, heads sprouting twigs. Just looking at them made cold dread pool in my stomach.

"There's a reason I brought you here," he murmured.

"Other than thinking this is a great way to flirt?" I joked.

He smiled, his eyes shutting. His long, dark lashes kissed his cheekbones. "Trust me, I have other, better ways of flirting."

He traced the backs of his fingers down both of my shoulders, sending goose bumps washing down my flesh to my toes. All I wanted to do was fall onto him and brush my lips against his. It had been an entire day since we'd kissed. Much too long.

But he turned his attention away from me and pinned it to the watercolor paintings. He sifted through them until he found what he was looking for.

"This is a darkling," he told me. "What it looks like in its true form. The man that I met could put on a glamour; he could change his outward appearance. But this is what happened when he shed that outer layer of magic."

The creature was dark, almost black, with arms like ropes and fingers that curled into claws. From its head sprouted dark tendrils that almost looked like branches. They twisted into a thorny crown atop his head. But his eyes—they were the worst. They were black and soulless, making the entire creature appear demon possessed.

"A darkling," I repeated, my fingers brushing over the watercolor. "I've never heard of such a thing."

"They're a rare type of monster. The one that killed my parents is only one of two that I've ever encountered," he explained. "They are steeped in evil, overcome with darkness and sadness. Once they lose themselves to that darkness, their humanity disappears, and this is what they become. There are other monsters that are similar to them—a withering is one. But I don't know much about those. No one does."

A shudder ran through me. The depths of gloom that Grim captured in the eyes of the creature was impossible to explain. I felt that if I stared too long, that I would fall victim to the same sadness that had eaten its soul.

"Why are you showing me this?"

"Because." He pinned the picture to a corkboard above the desk. "Becoming a darkling happens in stages. It doesn't take a person over all at once. While that person is changing, there are clues, symptoms so to speak."

I had a bad feeling about what he was going to say next. "And the clues in this one?"

"One of them is an oily substance. It can look like spilled gasoline on a tarmac, making it hard to detect. Unless you know what you're looking for."

I had a serious case of the willies dancing along my spine. I really, really did not like where this was going. "And have you seen that recently?"

My stomach clenched just asking the question. That clenching became an all-out twinge of pain when Grim nodded. "Yes, I did."

"When did you see it?"

His eyes sparkled darkly when he answered, "Tonight. At the crime scene where Newman was killed."

CHAPTER 11

I wanted to jump from my skin. "At the crime scene? Where Newman's car exploded?"

Grim nodded, *well*, grimly. "The spot was beside the vehicle. It looked like spilled fuel, as if someone had poured gas on the grass. But when I inspected closer, I knew what it was—darkling sign."

I raked my fingers through my hair, trying to work all of this out. "Okay, so someone made Newman's car explode, and you're saying it was a monster? This means a lot of things would have to have been set into place. First, the monster, or darkling, would have to know where Newman would need to be parked in order to have left its slime or whatever at the crime scene."

"Maybe not. It could've been there earlier to check it out."

I frowned, unconvinced. "I don't know; that seems awfully coincidental."

"The slime happens in the later stages of the darkling. It's almost like a dog leaving its scent behind. It's compulsory. That makes these creatures easier to track."

"And you've tracked them before." Not that it gave me much comfort, knowing what that one darkling had done to his parents. "And you're sure about this? That it's a darkling?"

He gazed at me with eyes full of sadness. "It is. That's why I wanted to take you someplace safe. Darklings are loners."

I scoffed. "Well, that's perfect, because the three assassins or friends of Newman that he showed us at the bar all looked like loners."

Concern flared in Grim's eyes. "Tell me everything."

And so I did. He pulled me to a couch (yes, in his armory) and we sat and chatted. I explained how each of the people looked and what their specialties were, though I never understood Herman's unless he was going to beat you in a reading contest.

"I'll track them down tomorrow," Grim told me. "In the meantime you need to be careful. My guess is that this darkling was only interested in killing Newman. But if the creature becomes provoked, then it will lash out against others."

I smiled widely. "You don't have to worry about me. Now that the money is gone and Cammie's off the hook, my life is getting back to normal. I've got a book to finish and a Pam to find."

"The Pam that Al told you to stay away from?"

"I have to find her for Snow, the ghost. The Heronomous spell book is still missing. We've got to locate it." A thought flared bright in my head. "What if...what if the darkling came from the book?"

He frowned. "Then someone would have to be using it, making the darkling do their bidding. That's a big coincidence, because the book has been missing for several weeks and Newman only just arrived in town."

I nibbled the tip of my finger. He was right. It didn't make a lot of sense.

"However," Grim added, "darklings can be controlled. A person could spell them to do their bidding."

"But what about the vehicle exploding?"

"I'll have to think about that. But be careful. This creature can't infect another person unless they get close enough to touch them and inject them with one of their spores. You'll know a darkling when you see it."

I shuddered.

He took my hand and ran his finger over the lines that cut across my palm. "The means of staying safe are easy. Lock your doors at night. Darklings can't go where they're not invited."

"Oh, like vampires?"

"No," he replied in a husky voice. "That's a myth about vampires." He studied my hand as he spoke. "Don't roam at night unless you're with me. I'll find this monster and stop it from hurting anyone else. Though you need to take precautions, I don't know that you have anything to fear. From what I already suspect, the creature intended to hurt Newman specifically."

That didn't make me feel any better. Just knowing that it was out there, possibly in my town, made me feel unsafe. But instead of getting all worried and silly, I just nodded. I was a big girl. I could take care of myself.

"Is there anything else I should know about the darkling?"

"Just be careful. The creature has to reveal itself in order to harm you. You'll see it coming. They tend to be loud."

Darkness crossed Grim's face, and I squeezed his hand. "What is it?"

His eyes flickered to mine, and he shook his head as if that would brush the cobwebs away. "It's nothing. I just want you to be safe, is all. If I could keep you here, I would. You can stay with me until we find it."

My heart jumped into my throat. "This from the man who doesn't want to commit?"

His eyes narrowed. "I never said that."

"Yes, you did."

"No, I didn't," he snarled.

His tone made me jump. In fact, it made me angry. I knew what I'd heard. "When you were talking about your old girlfriend, the one who almost killed you, you said that you didn't want commitment."

He threw his head back and laughed. Embarrassment burned at my cheeks. Had I misunderstood what he'd said? Impossible. He'd all but announced it, proclaimed it from the rafters.

He cupped my chin in his fingers and pulled me to him. Grim's lips brushed my eyelids (which I'd closed) and then my nose. He spoke as his mouth caressed my face.

"If I said anything about that, I was talking about before."

"Before what?" I murmured as his lips danced over mine. It was impossible to concentrate. What were we discussing again? "What was that?"

"I was saying *before* I met you. You enrage me because you don't listen. You are annoyingly headstrong and put yourself in trouble."

"*I* listen."

"You didn't when that *aghash* attacked."

That was ages ago. He was still thinking about that? But a creature had attacked us, and I'd only been trying to help him.

"You didn't listen, did you?"

Oh! Grim was talking again. It was futile to try thinking on my own while his lips grazed my skin.

"No, I didn't listen. But I did heal you."

"And you won my heart in doing so."

Wait. What? I pulled back. "What did you say?"

He smiled bashfully. Grim, bashful? What was this world coming to? But there it was. Red tinged his cheeks, and the smile quirking his mouth definitely looked shy.

"I said that you won my heart."

My own skipped several beats. Hope it didn't keep that up or else I'd need to hit the old emergency room. "I have?"

Yes, it was a terrible reply, but the only thing I could come up with.

Grim ran his hands behind my neck. "What is it that you've been missing this whole time? I made the pool because you inspire me. You fill my heart with happiness."

"But you...the whole commitment thing." Why did I keep beating a dead horse? "You said..."

"You misinterpreted my words," he growled. His lips brushed over my cheek. "I'm telling you how I feel. I haven't met anyone in a long, long time that I care for this much."

My heart inflated with joy. Grim wanted to be with me as much as I wanted to be with him. There was no need to run away and hide from it. There was no need to scurry in the other direction. Ever since I'd arrived in Willow Lake, I'd been clinging to the fear that I wouldn't live up to Grim's expectations. That he'd steal my heart and I'd be left more alone than when I started. But here he sat telling me that he felt the same way about me that I felt about him. That he wanted to be with me and that there wasn't a reason to fear any longer.

"Thank you," I murmured.

"For what?"

I sat back and drank in all his masculine beauty—the dark hair that tumbled over his shoulders, those hazel eyes, shining like polished gemstones, the calloused fingers roughly grazing my skin. I took all of him in and smiled.

"What are you thanking me for?" he asked again, skepticism in his voice.

"I'm thanking you for being vulnerable."

He rolled his eyes. "Let's not get carried away."

"Too frou-frou for you?"

He grunted.

I took that as a yes. "Well," I said in a teasing voice, "how about I thank you instead for taking a chance on me, for being willing to open your heart to risk."

There, he smiled. His palm slid over my cheek, and he pulled me in for a kiss. It started slowly and quickly deepened. The last time we'd become this heated, we were in his backyard working magic and I was ready to start throwing my clothing off.

This time, things moved a bit more slowly. Grim nuzzled my neck, and every girlie part I had sang with happiness. After a few minutes enduring ripples of pleasure washing over my body and knowing that nothing more would happen, our lips parted and we sat, foreheads touching and arms linked around one another.

Grim ran a finger over my mouth. "I should get you home."

"Do you have to?"

"I think so," he told me. "There are things worth waiting for, and this is one of them."

He just had to be the voice of reason, didn't he?

I didn't make a big deal of picking up my purse and heading back upstairs. His cellar was surprisingly cozy—for a place buried under the earth, that was.

I took another long look around and admired Grim's dedication to his profession. The weapons and collections of books told me that he was more than dedicated to hunting down monsters. This was his life. And if I wanted to be in it, I had to accept that.

As if reading my mind, he came up behind me and wrapped his arms around my waist. His chin dropped to my shoulder. "Do you think you can handle being involved with me? A hunter?"

"I'm assuming this is like being a policeman? You leave on calls, not knowing what you're going to find. It's going to be maddeningly frustrating, because I won't know if you're safe until you've finished a job. Monsters, like bad people, can ambush you. You could die at any moment."

Wow, the more I talked about it, the worse the images that flared in my mind.

Grim's hold on me tightened. "It is just like that, I'm sorry to say. I can't be sure, but I think that it wore on my mother."

"She probably worried so much about your father," I replied quietly.

Grim straightened and took me by the shoulders. He slowly turned me to face him, and he pulled me into a hug that made me forget everything. I buried my face in his chest and inhaled deeply. He smelled of soap and musk. I wanted to imprint this scent in my mind so that I'd never forget it, so I drank it up more.

"It's a lot that I'm asking," he said. "I wouldn't wish this on anyone. And that's one reason why I haven't gotten involved with a woman in a long time."

Jealousy snaked through my belly, and I slithered from his hold. "Are you saying that you *could* have gotten involved with someone else?"

He chuckled and pulled me back into his embrace. "No, I'm not saying that. I'm saying that I want to be with you. But there are risks, and you need to know them up front."

I understood that now. Grim could leave one day and never return. A creature could seek him out for revenge just as what had happened to his family. His life—and quite possibly mine by proximity—were in danger.

But as his arms held me tenderly, his body spoke its own language. It whispered of fondness, attachment, endearment, passion and even loyalty. Grim would be loyal. If I chose to walk down this path with him, then I would be protected by him. That, I knew. I just had to be willing to jump.

My heart fluttered. Yes, I was afraid. We weren't committing to marriage or anything, but openly giving him my heart was a big step—

for both of us. We'd each been wounded, our hearts sliced in two, and now we had the opportunity to mend them—together.

We only had to be willing to take the risk.

I tipped my head up to him and stared into his eyes. "I want to be with you and only you. You make my heart full." He kissed me again then, his lips making more promises. When we pulled away, I smiled. "Now. What do we do next?"

CHAPTER 12

Turned out the next thing was me going home. Drat. As much as I wanted to stay, I needed to check in on my sister. Cammie, it turned out, was snoring softly when I arrived at the cabin.

I tiptoed by her and headed into my room. I quietly changed and readied for bed. It seemed to take forever to fall asleep, but when I did, my dreams were filled with images of Grim.

I awoke the next day to find sunshine piercing my blinds. It was a bright, wonderful day. The world was a perfect, beautiful place, where only good things could happen.

Well, that was how I felt. I threw on a robe and headed into the main room to make myself a cup of coffee.

I was humming when I opened my bedroom door. The aroma of coffee filled the room, and Cammie lay on the couch, her legs stretched out in front of her, mug of steaming joe nestled between her hands.

"Well, look who's awake. What time did you get in last night?"

"Must've been around midnight." I pulled a mug from the cabinet and poured the rich, brown liquid into it and added a short pour of cream. "You were asleep when I got home."

"Yeah, all that excitement exhausted me." She ran her fingers through her dyed ebony locks. "But I tell you what, for the first time I slept like a baby."

"That's nice," I replied, not really listening to her. My mind instead was still brimming with thoughts of Grim.

I walked over to where she sat, and Cammie dropped her legs to the floor. "You seem awfully happy."

"I am."

She cocked a brow. "Oh? Things go good with Mr. Hot Stuff?"

"You could say that. We've decided to be together."

Cammie rolled her eyes. "Are y'all, like, going together, like we did in high school?"

"Are you making fun of me?"

"Not at all. But"—she rose and stretched her arms over her head, revealing a belly button ring that I hadn't noticed before—"now that the whole Newman thing is done over with, I've decided to stay a couple of days and then head out, get back to my old life."

This was great news! I'd been writing with Cammie at the house, but honestly I worked better in solitude. "Since you only have a few more days, what would you like to do?"

She smiled. "I want to go skinny dipping in the lake at midnight."

I started to laugh, but then I noticed the serious expression etched on her face. This was a problem because Grim had told me to stay in at night, to lock my doors.

"Um, it's too cold for all of that."

"Nonsense," she told me. "Folks in cold countries do it all the time in winter."

"Well, it's not winter yet, but the season is changing. Besides, aren't you talking about people who put on their *bathing suits* and take a dip in the hot springs?"

She flicked her hand, dismissing my concern. "Same thing. But I want to do it tonight. What do you say?"

"How about we go fishing instead?"

She deflated but still managed a weak smile. "Sure. Let's do that."

Snow was nowhere to be found that morning, so I couldn't tell her about the roadblocks that I'd hit in searching for Pam. It was probably a good thing that she wasn't here. I didn't want to have to tell her that finding Pam was turning out to be harder than I had originally thought it would be.

I showered and changed. Cammie was scrolling on her phone when I emerged from my room, ready to go. Tears rolled down her face.

Concern for my sister welled up inside my chest like a fist pressing on my rib cage. I rushed over to her and sat, touching her arm.

"Cammie, are you okay? What's wrong?"

She stared at the screen for a second and then lifted it for me to see. Taking up most of the slick surface was a picture of her and Newman. They each smiled widely for the camera, their heads touching, arms around one another.

I couldn't hide my confusion when I said, "This is what's upsetting you?"

She nodded dumbly. "We were so happy then. Newman may have been a sack of crap as a person, but in our early days he was great. We had so much fun together. He didn't deserve to die, Paige."

Are you sure about that? "I'm sorry for what happened to him, too. But you weren't upset like this last night."

She gulped down a sob. I handed her a tissue, and she blew her nose, hard. "I was hiding my true feelings," she explained. "But the more I thought about it, the more I've come to realize how crushed I am. I'm in mourning, Paige. I'm sad and I can't even go see his body because Newmie's been charred to a crisp."

Newmie? Now Cammie was using pet names for the man who would've killed her if he hadn't retrieved the money that she had stolen because he was cheating on her?

I rubbed her shoulder. "Come on. Why don't we go fishing, like we planned? We'll have fun. We'll rent a boat and just try to forget about what happened. If it makes you feel better, we can contact the police and see if they know anything about Newman's funeral arrangements."

Cammie nodded again, this time with a touch more life. "Whatever you say."

We got ourselves together and headed to the lake. It was a glorious day. Diamonds of sunlight lay scattered across the surface of Willow Lake, breaking apart only when a boat cut through the water.

At the rental place, we paid for a man take us out on his boat. We spent a couple of hours casting but didn't have any luck. Still, Cammie smiled some, which made my heart feel lighter. I understood her original anger at Newman. He'd cheated on her. But grief was a tricky thing. Even if you didn't expect to feel anything, it could still grip you by the throat unexpectedly. That was what Cammie was experiencing.

When the short excursion was finished, we grabbed a Coke from the rental shop and walked around the lakefront. Though the weather was turning chilly and the kids had all returned to school, there were still plenty of people enjoying the splendors of the area—tall pines, good fishing, camping.

We were walking when Cammie's hand shot out and gripped my arm. *Hard.* I flinched. "What are you…why are you doing that?"

"Look, Paige. Ain't that the blade guy?"

What was she talking about? "What blade guy?"

"The one Newman called his associate."

My gaze followed hers and latched onto a thin blond man resting his hip on a picnic table. He wore dark sunglasses, and he watched the water as if he was trying to absorb its arcane knowledge or something stupid like that.

Cammie's face became stony with anger. "I'm going to have a chat with him."

Before I could stop her, my sister was scurrying over to Stanislav, the Russian.

She wagged her finger in his face. "I need a word with you."

Stanislav slowly turned toward Cammie. "Yes?"

"Did you kill Newman?"

I wanted to smack my forehead. You didn't just go asking people if they committed murder. It wasn't as if they would admit to it.

"No," he replied without a Russian accent, which surprised me so much that I commented on it.

"You don't sound Russian."

Stanislav slowly pulled off his sunglasses. His eyes were ice blue, and just locking gazes with him made a shiver quake through my body.

"My parents are from Russia. I'm from here. So no, I don't have an accent."

"Why'd Newman die?" Cammie said accusingly.

"My, what a sharp knife you have," I replied in a hard voice, nodding my head toward the blade in his hand. Cammie saw what I was staring at, and she rolled her eyes. *Time for me to take over.* "What my sister means is that she's very upset about Newman's death."

Stanislav's pale gaze landed on Cammie. "Now you don't have to worry about the money. Whoever killed him did you a favor. I would leave it at that."

He pushed off the table and started to walk away, but Cammie was having none of it. "Look, someone killed him. Someone *killed* Newman. No, he wasn't the best guy on the block. Far from it. But he had the opportunity to hurt me and didn't. He could've made me pay for stealing his money, but instead he brushed it off. Not many others woulda done that."

Stanislav stopped and shifted his weight. He glanced over his shoulder and shot us a bored look. "He hired me in case he needed backup. I'm sure same as the others. He was trying to make amends with me, I'm sure."

My ears pricked at that. "Amends? For what?"

The knife wielder slowly turned around, flicking the knife open and shut. The blade glinted in the sun as it repeatedly sheathed and unsheathed. Stanislav moved his hand so quickly that I wondered if this was a not so thinly veiled threat.

"Make amends for sleeping with my wife," he told us coldly. "Newman had an affair. When I found out, I nearly killed him, but he promised me money. We were poor, my wife and I. Work had dried up. I was a factory man. But after I met Newman, I went into…another business. We've been doing well ever since. From time to time Newman calls to ask me to come help him with situations. Or at least he did." His gaze cut to the ground for a brief moment before alighting back on us. "When he called me the other day, promising that he'd compensate me well, I came aboard."

I frowned because something didn't make sense. "What about his boss?"

Stanislav shook his head. "There was no boss. Newman worked for himself. So that money was his. No one else is going to come looking for it."

Relief filled me as worry released its hold from my heart. Thank goodness. The last thing that I needed was a mafia boss exhorting money from me that I didn't have.

Cammie wagged a finger at him. "You expect me to believe that you didn't harbor ill feelings toward Newman for doing the nasty with your wife?"

Stanislav shrugged. "Believe whatever you feel like. I made my peace with my wife and Newman. But if you want someone who may have had more reason to be angry with Newman than me, you should talk to Pippa."

Cammie's face scrunched in confusion. "Pippa? Who's that?"

"The perfume lady." I nudged her with my elbow. "Remember?"

"Oh, right." She pinned her steely gaze on Stanislav. "So what? Did Newman break her heart, too?"

He sheathed the knife and slid it into his front pocket. "That's for her to tell. It's not my story. But I'm sure you can find her in town. No one's leaving, not until we know who did this. You see, Newman meant something to each of us, and even if one of us did kill him, we're all sticking around."

"To see that justice is done," I murmured.

"Something like that," he mumbled.

"One more question."

He gave me a heavy-lidded look. "Yeah?"

"Do you know anything about darklings?"

Stanislav's brows pinched together. "What are you talking about?"

I shook my head. "Never mind. It was a random question."

"Anything else?" His gaze flicked from me to Cammie. "If not, I need to get going."

We told him that we were done, and he stalked off. Though I'd originally not been interested in talking to him or even digging into the truth about Newman's death, now I was intrigued. I needed to know who or what had caused that explosion—and why.

Cammie snorted. "What in the world were you talking about—a darkling? Sounds like some sort of stupid magical thingamajig from *Lord of the Rings* or something. And you can be sure, I ever see any kind of creature, I'm pulling out my gun and shooting."

She started to dig the pistol from her purse, but I pushed her hand back down. "Okay. I got it. I totally understand. Sorry, I don't know what got into me."

"Dang right you don't know."

She started to walk off and my phone rang. It was Grim. I quickly answered. "Hello?"

"Hey, beautiful."

My heart melted. Correction—*I* melted. "Hey, gorgeous."

As in pure Grim fashion, he cut right to the chase. "I'm calling not only to hear your melodic voice, but to also tell you that I found out something about Pam."

I was still stuck on the fact that he'd used the word *melodic* before I realized he'd said something about Pam. "Oh, not about the darkling?" I whispered, dropping my voice so that Cammie wouldn't hear.

"I'm still working on that. But I've got information."

"Great. When can we meet up?"

I swore that I heard a smile stretch across his face. "How about now?"

"Perfect. Tell me where and I'll meet you."

CHAPTER 13

*J*raced home to see if Snow was around because I didn't want to meet Grim without her present. She needed to hear what he had to say about Pam, whether it be good or bad. But lately it seemed like Snow wasn't hanging around the cabin as much as she normally did.

Whatever *normal* was for a ghost.

"What do you think Grim's got to say?" Cammie asked as I dropped my purse on the dining table.

"No clue. He didn't even give one hint."

She smirked. "What kind of boyfriend is that? The sort that doesn't offer a clue?"

The next words flew from my mouth before I could stop them. "Who said anything about him being my boyfriend?" Jeez, how defensive could I sound?

"Oh, he's your boyfriend all right." Cammie flashed me a thousand-watt Cheshire cat smile. "You'll probably wind up married with a litter-full of kids."

"My kid making-days are over, thank you very much."

"Well, then you'll have hot whoopee for the rest of your lives."

I rolled my eyes. "Life is about more than whoopee."

"Is it, really?" She dropped onto the couch and draped her arms over the back of it. "Are you sure?"

Ignoring her, I searched the small cabin for my friendly neighborhood ghost. "Snow, are you here? Snow?" I found her lying on my bed, a ghostly book in her hands. "What are you reading?"

She yawned and stretched her delicate arms over her head. "Oh, just a book about what to expect in the afterlife."

I frowned. "Aren't you *in* the afterlife?"

"I certainly hope not. This is limbo, if anything." She pointed skyward. "Up there's where I'm supposed to be."

"Heaven. Right. Listen, about that—Grim has some information to tell me about Pam. Want to come?"

"Sure."

With all the body control of a ballerina, Snow gracefully pulled herself from my bed and followed me into the main room.

I hitched my purse to my shoulder. "We're going to talk to Grim."

Cammie waved from her spot in front of the TV. "Go on. I'm gonna stay here. All that fishing today made me tired."

"You sure?"

"Yep."

"Suit yourself." To Snow I said, "Let's go."

We were meeting Grim at the police station. He was doing some work on the Newman case and had apparently been tied up there all day. I couldn't help but think that had to do with the darkling. Why else would Grim have been needed? As we approached downtown Willow Lake, people were out shopping, meandering the streets with smiles stretched over their faces, the golden glow of the sun beaming down on them.

It was impossible not to think that perhaps one of these people was a darkling. From what Grim had explained, the creature could hide itself as a person.

A cold chill wrapped around my spine. The creature could be anyone.

That was if his theory about the oily stain found at the crime scene was correct. The substance could also have simply been some sort of starter fluid, placed there to help destroy Newman's vehicle.

I turned to Snow, and she stared out the window, her palm pressed to the glass. My stomach clenched. Here I was thinking about a mystery while she was obviously emotionally tortured.

"You okay?" I asked.

She inhaled sharply and turned to me as if suddenly remembering that I was in the car with her. "Yes, sorry. I was just thinking."

"About what?"

"Well,"—she rested her head on the glass. Not sure how, but she did. "I can't remember much about my family, right? I know that I had a husband. But…"

When she didn't continue for several seconds, I nudged her. "But what?"

She nibbled the tip of her finger. "But I'm worried about what we might find out. About me. About him. About my life."

We reached a stoplight, and I took a moment to study her. Snow was normally fairly blasé. She was one to roll with the punches. But the worry in her eyes made me pause.

"Snow, I'm doing this for you. You asked me to find out who had thrown you into the book. You said that Pam might know something." I didn't intend to sound accusatory, but that was exactly the tone of my voice, and I instantly regretted it. It made it worse that she winced at my words. "Sorry. I'm not trying to hurt your feelings, it's just that I'm confused. What's going on?"

The light turned and I drove on. Beside me, Snow sighed heavily, sinking down into her seat. "It's just that I have a feeling, it's more like a ball of worry, really, that I didn't mind being thrown into the book. That I was afraid of something or someone."

"Oh, I get it. I see now." We reached the police station, and I slid the vehicle into a parking spot out front. I put the car into park and rested my head on the seat. "Snow, if you don't want to know what happened, we don't have to pursue this. It's no big deal for me to tell Grim to forget it. But I get the feeling that if we don't, you'll be stuck in limbo a lot longer than you want to be."

She gazed at me with shy, worried eyes. "How much longer?"

"Does eternity sound like a number you're interested in hearing?"

"No."

I clicked my tongue. "Well shucks, because it's the only one I've got."

She stared out the windshield for so long that I thought she might back out, but after another moment Snow exhaled a gusty sigh and sat up. "All right. Let's go see what Grim has to say."

A smile curled on my face. "I think you've made the right decision."

Grim was waiting up front for me when I entered the station. The place smelled like lemon floor cleaner and cigarettes. Not sure how that combination worked out, given that the station was a smoke-free building, but perhaps the acrid scent was a holdover from the days when a person could light up inside.

I spotted Cowan and waved before Grim came over and escorted me back out. His hand rested on my lower back as he guided me to one of the break tables stationed on the side of the building.

"Is Snow here?" he asked.

"I'm here," Snow replied.

But Grim could neither see nor hear her. "She's beside me."

Grim scrubbed a hand down his cheek. "I will say, it was hard to get anyone to talk to Pam. But I went back to Al and asked him for the full story."

"Al owns a taco restaurant," I explained to Snow.

She didn't say anything, but her fingers twisted into her shirt. She worked the fabric into a knot as she watched Grim, her shoulders hunched with unease.

I wanted to reach over and take her hand to calm her. But you know, the whole transparent thing didn't work out in my favor.

So instead I focused on Grim. "What did Al say?"

Grim cleared his throat. "He told me an interesting story."

I quirked a brow, intrigued. "Do tell."

"Apparently when Pam first moved to that side of town, everyone loved her. She was well-liked in the community. Was always dropping off baked goods to her neighbors and offering to babysit their kids. She had a reputation as a grandmother type. People liked her."

"Let me guess," I told him. "At some point this goes wrong."

"Exactly." Grim's hazel eyes cut to me. "Pam started acting weird. Strange things started happening around her."

"What sort of things?"

"Pets began going missing."

The hairs on the back of my neck soldiered to attention. "That is creepy."

He nodded. "That was only the beginning."

Worry knotted my stomach. "Don't tell me that children started going missing."

"No, no." He lifted his palm in a stop gesture. "Nothing like that. But first it was the animals, and then people started seeing strange lights on at her house. Creepy, weird lights. And then the place began to smell. Reeked of evil, the way Al told it."

"How can a place reek of evil?" Snow asked.

Though Grim couldn't hear her, he might as well have been able, because he answered the question. "According to Al, the whole property took on a sulfur scent, like it was connected to hell."

Cold dread pooled in my stomach. "This doesn't sound good."

"It gets worse."

My eyes bulged. "How could it get worse?"

Grim smirked. "Just wait. Patience, my muse."

When he called me that, a ribbon of warmth flowed over me. I was his muse! Even though I wanted to curl into a ball on his lap, I stopped myself and listened.

Grim sat up and surveyed the people walking around us, his eyes narrowed. After taking a moment to do that, he brought his attention back to us.

"What is it?" I asked.

"Just watching," he told me as if that was explanation enough, which I supposed it was.

"Back to Pam."

"Right. There are the animals missing and now the smells. People are becoming suspicious of their neighbor. So several men got together, and they decided to visit good old Pam and find out what's really going on." Grim's jaw hardened, and I knew whatever he was going to tell me, that it had upset him. "When they arrived, at first Pam tried to brush off the smell. She played it off as if there was nothing wrong, but the men insisted that she let them in."

Suddenly I was uneasy. "Were they forceful?"

"Don't know. But they eventually got into the house."

"What did they find?" Snow asked, her ghostly fingers still knotting up her shirt, her knuckles white.

Grim drummed his fingers on the table. He didn't want to tell me what they found. His body language screamed it. He didn't even like what Al had told him, I realized.

I peered into his eyes that were fraught with worry. "It's okay. Whatever it is. I can handle it."

"The problem is that I'm still trying to process it," he explained.

Oh, that meant whatever he had to tell me, it must've been *badder* than bad. "I see."

He cleared his throat. "What the men found when they went inside were parts."

He paused and I frowned, not understanding. "Parts?"

"Body parts."

My jaw fell open. "What? Oh my gosh! People parts?"

"No," Grim said, his jaw jumping. "It wasn't that. Pam would've been arrested if that was the case. The men, at first, weren't even sure what they were seeing. They were so overcome by the sight of hairy legs and tentacle-laden arms that it took minutes for them to realize that they weren't staring at regular body parts."

It was then that it dawned on me exactly what Grim was saying, and I immediately understood *why* he was so bothered by Al's story.

"What was it?" Snow asked, clearly confused.

I took a deep breath, stilling my mind and doing my best to force out the disgusting image that Grim had just planted in it.

"They were monster parts," I told Snow. "Pam's house was full of dead monsters."

Grim nodded. "As soon as the men realized what was going on, they called the police to investigate. This was years ago, before I arrived in Willow Lake. But by the time the police arrived, all the pieces were gone, cleaned up. Pam, however, never lived down the rumors that flowed through Willow Lake after that. Word about what the men found spread like fire. No one trusted her after that."

"But she stayed?" I asked.

Grim nodded. "She did. Still lives out there, but no one will have anything to do with her."

I sat back, dragging my fingers along the top of the table. This was a lot to unpack. After a moment I said, "So what do we do now?"

Grim's eyes became smoldering emeralds. "We pay Pam a visit. If she's played with monsters before, she may have some answers for us."

CHAPTER 14

*W*e decided to ambush Pam (okay, so maybe *ambush* wasn't the right word) later during the day, when she would most likely be home.

Snow vanished after we met with Grim. She mumbled something about returning to the cabin and then left, quite literally disappearing right before my eyes.

"Well, I guess we're alone now," I told Grim sarcastically.

His lips coiled into a devilish grin. "What would you like to get up to?"

Was that a euphemism, or was that a *euphemism*? Meaning, did Grim's words have a double meaning?

Turned out, they didn't. "Until we know who the darkling is, you need to practice your magic," he told me in a firm voice.

"Sure."

He dropped his face into his hands, clearly annoyed with me. "I mean, *actually* practice, Paige. Not just throw some magic here and there. You need to know how to protect yourself."

"I know how to warm a cup of coffee. Does that count?"

"No," he said coldly. His eyes focused on me sharply, and I felt my insides wither. He must've realized what a stony look he was giving me, because his expression softened to one that made my heart inflate with happiness. Grim rose. "Come on. I'll help you. Let's go work out a little frustration."

"I'm not frustrated."

"I am," he growled.

"Oh, okay."

Not wanting to tick him off any more than he obviously already was, I followed Grim to his fancy new vehicle and climbed inside.

We rode in silence until he turned down the road that led to his house. I expected him to stop when we reached his cottage, but instead Grim kept right on driving, rumbling down a path that wound behind his home.

We reached a locked gate with a privacy fence surrounding it. Grim pushed a button on a small box attached to his visor, like a garage opener, and the gate swung open. Behind the fence lay a meadow that had recently been cut. Yellowing grass lay in thick clumps atop the earth, and behind the meadow was a line of pines. They had been planted in a row and reminded me of a wall.

He parked and came over to open my door.

"Stay beside me," he instructed.

"Okay," I replied slowly, wondering why he was being so cryptic. I slowly exited the vehicle, taking in the yellowing grass and the tall pines. "This place is beautiful."

He grunted. Typical Grim response. "It's also deadly."

The hairs on the back of my neck sprang up. "What?"

He turned to me for the first time since we'd arrived and said softly, "I'm not going to let anything happen to you."

I felt his voice all the way to my bones. He was like that, able to reach all the way to my soul, it felt, with his words or the expression in his eyes. I believed him, too. Grim would not let anything happen to me.

The weight of that statement sank into me. It was the meaning behind it that I understood. Grim wasn't just letting his heart be open; he was ready to hand it to me.

And I was willing to take it and hold it close, protecting such a fragile gift.

I licked my lips, preparing for whatever was to come. Grim's eyes trailed my mouth, and heat sprang to my cheeks.

Perhaps it wasn't the best time for this whole seduction thing to be happening.

"I'm ready to train," I said in a hoarse whisper.

His gaze cut to the field, and he pinned his attention on the task at hand. "I created this training area."

I quirked a brow. All I saw was an open field and trees in the distance. There was nothing that suggested this was a training facility.

"All right," I said skeptically.

He smiled and amusement danced in his eyes. "Let me show you." Grim pushed up his sleeves. "Stand back."

I wasn't sure how far back I should go, but I decided to err on the side of caution and put myself about ten feet away from Grim.

This gave me a fantastic view of Grim's perfect back. His shoulders tightened and he opened his hands. Electricity crackled and popped at the end of his fingertips, sending a fissure of worry shooting to my toes. What kind of training had I gotten myself into?

Grim took a step forward, and a black figure shot up from the ground. It looked like a cardboard werewolf, with thick dark fur and a snarling face. The thing was made of either silicone or rubber and was covered in patchy fur.

Electricity shot from Grim's fingers, entangling the wolf. The magic popped and the werewolf sank back into the earth.

Okay, so that wasn't so bad. I could handle this sort of obstacle course. No problem.

Grim took several more steps, and a picture of a gray-robed witch flipped up from the ground. From her extended fingers shot nets infused with magic. Grim cut them down easily, his magic slicing through the webbing, sending it falling in strands to the earth.

All right, once again, I thought that I could manage to defeat the witch. Then a knot balled up in my throat. *Maybe.*

The witch disappeared and Grim took several more steps into the meadow. I wondered what would pop up next. Would it be a troll? A goblin? An evil fairy?

Though all were good guesses, I supposed, the obstacle that roared from the earth sent a wave of fear pulsing over my skin.

A structure made of wood erupted from the ground, and a tremble quaked over the meadow. The thing had three levels and each level did something different.

The bottom level spun, sending balls of magic flying through the air. The second level moved counterclockwise. It was peppered with sharp spikes that slashed the sky. Get too close to those and you'd be sliced to ribbons.

At the very top sat a red cone that simply spun in time with the rest of the thing.

With lightning speed, Grim raced toward the wooden structure. He dodged balls of magic as they torpedoed toward him. Using catlike reflexes that I didn't know Grim had, he jumped onto one of the spikes and shot a line of magic into the red cone.

The structure groaned to a stop, and I stared, my jaw on the ground. Was I supposed to do that? Did he think that my middle-aged body could run and jump like a WNBA player? There was no way on God's green earth that I'd be able to do anything like that.

Grim strode back toward me. He wasn't even breaking a sweat. How was that possible? If I'd run and thrown magic, there would be so much under-boob sweat to deal with that I would've been praying for a sports bra.

"Impressive," I murmured, hoping that if I stroked his ego hard enough that he wouldn't say the two words I dreaded hearing.

"Your turn."

Crap. He said the words.

I brushed my hand over his bulging bicep. "Oh, you are very funny."

"Paige," he replied, a serious glint in his eyes, "I'm not kidding. You're going to do this."

"I can't do that, that, *thing*." A nervous laugh bubbled from my chest. "There's no way that I can deal with that monstrosity. You jump like a basketball player. I don't jump."

"You'll do a modified version," he replied, running his fingers encouragingly down my arm. "I'll be right beside you."

And he kept his promise. Grim placed his body directly behind mine, guiding me with his hands and every other part of him as the werewolf sprang from the ground. He directed my magic, showing me how to aim quickly and to hit with deadly accuracy.

"Good," he said, brushing his lips over my cheek. "Now let's do something harder."

I kept my mouth shut, not even joking about anything that could have been harder.

If you catch my drift.

The witch was next with her nets infused with magic. The first one hit me square in the chest, sending pain raining through my body.

"Oh," I yelped, falling to the ground.

Grim held me tight. "If you want to stop, we can."

I gritted my teeth. This was war now. No inanimate object was going to best me. I hardened my jaw and took the hand that Grim offered.

"I can do it," I told him.

"You're sure?"

I nodded hard. "I've got this."

I approached the witch again, with Grim close behind. She threw the first net, and even though every time she cast one, it was thrown from a different angle, I was ready.

I threw electricity at her. I drew on the power that I absorbed from Grim and tossed it right back at the witch. This time my magic connected with the net, and it fell in strands to the ground.

I jumped in celebration. "I did it!"

I turned and threw my arms around Grim's neck. His own arms tightened around me. I hadn't completed the course, no, but it was a start.

It felt good to be standing in Grim's strong arms, to feel his hands tighten on my spine. I pulled back and stared up into his eyes. Grim glanced down at me, his own eyes beaming.

"Are you proud of me?" I teased.

He chuckled, his gaze darting to the ground. "Almost. That was hard. But not as hard as the pillar."

"Oh, is that what you call that monstrosity of death?"

He laughed again. "That's what I call it. But you don't have to attempt it. It's hard, and it took me months to beat."

"It did? But you raced up it like the challenge was no big deal," I said, remembering how he'd zipped lightly all the way to the top. "You made it look easy."

"Trust me, it isn't." He looked over my shoulder and nodded. "Want a go?"

I turned around to take in the structure. The spikes looked even more intimidating when they weren't moving. Their points were sharp as needles, ready to rip into my clothes—or flesh.

Grim wrapped his arms around me, and I sank into his body, feeling his chin rest on my shoulder. "I could stay like this," I told him, fully telling the truth.

"But then you'd never know if you could beat the pillar."

I scoffed. "It took you months to best it. What makes you think I'll be able to do it in one sitting?"

"You won't."

I peeled myself off him, furious. "Why are you even suggesting it, then?"

He folded his arms. "To give you a goal, something to reach for. Let's face it, at some point you're leaving, Paige. You're not staying here forever."

His words smacked me in the face. "Yes, it's only a rental. The book is almost finished."

And I didn't have anyplace to go. My old house was gone, sold, and I was only renting the cabin for three months. Months that were quickly whizzing by. What would I do once the lease was up? I could stay on, probably. But I didn't want to live in a tiny cabin at the lake forever. I needed to finish the book and get it sold so that I'd have some money coming in.

Grim grazed his thumb over my cheek, sending shivers dancing over my flesh. "I've only just found you. I'm not sure that I'm ready to let you go."

"So you want me to tackle the impossible pillar in the hope that the challenge will make me want to stay?"

He smirked. "Something like that."

I wrapped my arms around him and rested my head on his shoulder. "Fighting that pillar isn't going to make me want to stay. *You* will," I whispered, almost afraid to say it. But it was true, and since Grim was being open and honest with his feelings, I would be, too.

He gently tipped my face to his and slowly kissed me. "What am I going to do with you, my muse?"

I grinned at the mention of my nickname. "How about you put me in your pocket and take me everywhere you go?"

He chuckled. "How about we enjoy one another?"

"That too."

He kissed me again before slowly spinning me around. "All right. It's time to try the pillar."

I groaned. "I thought I'd gotten out of this."

"Nope. Go on. Give it one good go."

The scary structure groaned to life. It turned slowly at first, but quickly picked up speed until it reached what I liked to think of as *deadly velocity.*

I fisted my hands and gritted my teeth. "All right. I'm ready for this. Time to kick some wood butt."

CHAPTER 15

*A*ll it took was one good whack from the side of a sharp point and I called it a day. It hurt, but nothing was broken. It wasn't Grim's fault, either. He guided me like a pro, telling me when to approach the pillar. But the spikes freaked me out (and rightly so). I hesitated, and that was when I got whacked.

Grim drove me back to my car, and I went on home. There I found Cammie eating ice cream from a carton and watching *Days of Our Lives.*

"Is that show still on?" I asked.

"Oh yeah." She spoke through a mouthful of chocolate chip. "It's almost over. Give me five minutes and then I'll be all yours."

To do what with, I didn't know. But that was fine. Grim's obstacle course had left me sweaty, so I took a quick shower and decided to go the distance and wash my hair. Though I dyed my graying locks a deep brown, they were a pain to dry and smooth, wanting to poke out everywhere and not cooperate.

But after about forty-five minutes of working on my hair, I got it presentable enough to be seen in public. Cammie was cleaning up the kitchen when I emerged from the bathroom.

"You ready?" she asked.

"Ready for what?" Had I missed something? Had we planned to go out and about town?

She scoffed like I should've known *for what.* "To find that Pippa lady. We got to ask her questions about Newman. Look here, I made a chart."

She pointed to the kitchen table. Taped to it was a small piece of white copy paper that had been cut down and a stick-figure face was drawn over it. Above the picture was the word *Stanislav.*

I peered at it to make sure that I was seeing what I thought I was seeing. "Is that supposed to be a drawing of Stanislav?"

"Yeah, this is my suspect board."

"But it's a table."

She shrugged as if to say, *That's a pesky detail.* "Look here, I've written how Stanislav's wife cheated on him with Newman. If that's not motive to kill, I don't know what is."

"But he seemed to be over it," I countered.

Cammie crossed her arms, and her bloodred nails dug into her biceps. "That's what he said, but you know as well as I do that you cain't trust no man when they say that. Stanislav would've wanted revenge. You can be sure of it."

"Mm. I don't know. He didn't seem to care too much."

She threw up her arms in frustration. "Why am I even talking to you about this? You don't get it."

Once again, a reason why my sister and I couldn't be friends after this. She raced ahead without really looking and listening to what was being said to her.

But instead of arguing, I sighed. "I don't get what?"

"What I'm saying—the man had motive."

"To do what? Stick a pipe bomb in Newman's gas tank? First of all, we watched all three people emerge from the trees when Newman called them. We didn't see anybody come back out and plant something in his car. For all we know, the bomb was placed inside to activate when Newman put his vehicle in reverse. It could've been there earlier, planted by someone we didn't even see."

Not to mention the fact that Grim was convinced a darkling was involved.

"That's why we gotta go track this Pippa down, see what she knows."

I glanced out the window. The sun was low in the sky. Darkness would swallow the earth in a few hours. If we were going to be out, we needed to be so now, not later.

"Okay, but we've got to hurry."

"Why?" she asked, her brows pinched in suspicion.

"Because…I've got plans with Grim. We're going to talk to Pam later." Which was true but not the whole truth. "So I need to get back here."

"You can always meet him out and I can bring the car home."

"No, that won't work."

"Why not?"

"It just won't." I grabbed my purse and threw it over my shoulder. "Do you have any idea where this Pippa is going to be?"

Cammie's eyes glittered with mischief. "Now, where do you think we'd find a woman who likes to smell good?"

"I have no idea."

Cammie took my arm. "Come on, I'll show you."

After expending so much energy with Grim, I was understandably a bit tired and very relaxed. Almost like after-having-a-massage level of relaxation. But I let Cammie drag me through Willow Lake until we reached a strip mall with several clothing boutiques.

"I bet she's here," Cammie told me, her hand washing over my windshield. "A woman like that enjoys shopping. No doubt about it."

"You think so?" I was skeptical, but there was no need to crush my sister's spirit, so I didn't argue the point to excess. "Well, we can go in and see."

The first boutique turned out to be a letdown. There was no sign of Pippa. But I had to admit that I was entranced by the clothes. If I'd actually had money, I would've grabbed several blouses. One was a beautiful shade of cream with long flouncy sleeves. It was a perfect date shirt.

"She ain't here," Cammie grumped. "Come on."

It took all my will power to follow her out. As soon as we stepped outside, my phone chirped. It was my agent, Madeleine.

I shooed Cammie on. "I'll catch up."

She disappeared into the next shop as I answered my phone. "Madeleine, I'm so glad you called."

"Darling, it's been ages. How's the book coming?"

"It's great," I said, meaning it. "It's almost done. I should have it to you by next week."

She sighed with relief. "Oh, wonderful. I tell you, Paige, this is it. This is the book that's going to get your career up and running again. Your publisher already loves what she's read. You'll do the whole PR circuit again—talk shows, morning shows, the works. Everyone has forgotten about that little disaster a while back. People's memories are short, my dear. Very short when there's always a new person that the media wants us to despise."

My stomach clenched. I'd be doing the PR circuit? Of course, I was used to doing it before, but now Grim was in my life. Things in Willow Lake were quiet, and I liked that. I'd had fancy cars and a fancy home. Right now all I wanted to do was relax, take things one day at a time.

"Paige, are you there?" Madeleine asked.

"Yes, I'm here."

"Good. Send me the pages as soon as they're done. I'll be looking forward to reading."

Before I could say another word, she hung up, leaving me standing on the sidewalk, wondering how to marry my old life with my new one.

While I was debating how to tell Madeleine that I didn't want to do the PR junket, a car pulled into the parking lot. A woman stepped out. She wore all black—heels, dress, even a black hat. She opened the door to one of the boutiques and disappeared inside.

A pulse of excitement flashed in my body. It was Pippa. I scanned the shops, trying to remember which one Cammie had vanished into.

Turned out, I didn't have to guess because right then a door swung open and Cammie stepped out, cursing like a sailor. "What the heck? I know my sixth sense is always right. That woman is here somewhere. I dang sure know it."

"Cammie!" I rushed over to her, stuffing my phone back in my purse. "She's here. Just pulled up."

My sister's face broke out in a wide smile. "She is?"

"Yes. Come on." I dragged her to the door that Pippa had gone through. Before I opened it, I gave Cammie a stern look. "Now, be cool. Whatever you do, do not run in there accusing anyone of murder."

She scoffed. "I ain't gonna do that. Have I ever just accused someone of killing another?"

"Yes. You did that to Stanislav."

"Well, he looked guilty," she spat. "And if this woman looks guilty, I'm gonna do the same to her. In fact—"

I interrupted her by opening the door. "There's no time to keep chatting. Come on."

The inside of the store looked like a jungle had exploded. Tall potted palms sat in chubby cerulean blue vases just beyond the door. The sound of trickling water filled the shop, and the smell of thick spicy incense floated throughout the interior.

The wares were exotic masks, glass lamps with colorful jewel-tone plates of leaded glass, and gilded jewelry. I regretted, but at the same time was grateful that I hadn't visited this store before, because I would easily have spent every last dime in it.

Cammie coughed and swatted at a smoky line of incense. "Ah, new-age crap! Where'd she go?"

I pulled her deeper into the store until we found Pippa standing by a wall of African tribal masks.

"Follow my lead," I murmured to Cammie, praying that she did as I asked.

When we reached Pippa, I pretended to study the wall and then looked over and elbowed Cammie. "Hey, don't I know you?" I asked Pippa.

She looked over lazily, her gaze starting at my head before dragging to my feet and back up to meet my eyes. "I was wondering when you'd find me."

"We *need* to find you," Cammie spat. "Did you kill Newman?"

Once again, there were no tactics here. Or at least she'd used the wrong ones. I smiled tightly at my sister. "What she means is, it's so horrible about what happened to Newman, isn't it?"

"Is it?" Pippa turned back to the masks. "I'm not so sure. He wasn't a good man." She glanced over at Cammie. "You should know that."

"But he didn't deserve to die," Cammie snapped.

Pippa shrugged, clearly not caring. "Maybe he didn't. Maybe he did."

"Why'd you come to work for him?" I asked her.

"If you must know—"

"We must," Cammie said, stepping closer to Pippa. "We have to know."

96

Pippa rolled her eyes and scoffed. "Look, if I was guilty, I would already be gone. Though I can understand why you'd think I had something to do with it."

"Yeah, you would." Cammie paused. "Why's that?"

"Well, someone must've told you about how Newman screwed me over in that smelling contest."

Cammie's expression fell. "The what? Come again?"

Pippa exhaled hard. "The smelling competition. It's a big deal—an annual contest. The goal is to knock a person out with a fragrance. Of course, I had mine—sulfur and salt, perfect combination." She smiled wistfully and I almost puked. Then a dark shadow crossed Pippa's face. "That was until Newman stepped in. He walked over to the person we were supposed to knock out and broke wind in his face. The man fell off his chair, passing out instantly. Needless to say, I didn't win."

This was so confusing. "So Newman beat you out in a stink contest?"

"It's much more prestigious than it sounds."

"Right."

"Like I said," Pippa told us, "if I had killed him, I would've split. I didn't like Newman. In fact, when he knocked that person out, I was so angry. But at the same time I respected him." Tears welled in her eyes. "You can say that I had a soft spot for him."

From her reaction, it was clear to me that she and Newman had dabbled in a relationship. Yuck. What was it with that guy? He wasn't even good-looking, but he'd managed to seduce all these women—my sister included.

"So no," she said emphatically, "I didn't kill him. But if you find out who did, let me know."

Cammie, not one to give things up, said with a self-righteous smirk, "You sure about that? The killing part," she added quickly, for clarification.

"I'm sure," Pippa answered. "Have a good one and let me know what you find out."

"How will we find you?" I asked.

"Oh, I'll be around."

Pippa turned and walked away, leaving us standing in the shop.

When she opened the door, her purse flipped up, revealing the soft leather underside. There, streaked down the center, was a long line of what looked like oil.

If I hadn't known any better, I would've said that it looked like darkling sign.

CHAPTER 16

"*S*o Newman farted better than her and that made the knife guy think Pippa would want to kill Newman?" Cammie mused while I drove us back to the house.

"I guess so," I murmured, wondering the same thing. I wasn't interested in getting sucked into the mystery of who killed Newman because I simply didn't care, but Grim was involved. And let's face it, I didn't want him to get hurt. "But she also had an affair with Newman."

And a dark, oily substance on the bottom of her bag. I needed to tell Grim about that, but not with Cammie around.

"Oh yeah, they did the nasty. I knew that look on her face." My sister stretched and grazed her fingernails over the felt lining the car's ceiling. "So. What're we up to now?"

"Now I'm taking you home. Grim tracked down Pam, and we're going over to her house to talk to her."

She folded her arms in annoyance. "Why do I have to stay home?"

"Because it's…a great TV night."

"No, it ain't. I already checked the TV Guide."

"You still read TV Guide?" Who read that anymore with all the streaming services available?

"Yes, I do. So I'm coming with you."

She couldn't come with us because Pam knew about magical

monsters and creatures. Cammie didn't, and had made her stance on what she would do to magical beings very clear.

"Cammie, I don't think it's a good idea. Not this time. I'm sorry." I said all of this in my most sympathetic voice. "Can I get a rain check?"

She dropped her arms to her sides limply. "What am I supposed to do with myself, then? I know! I'll call Ferguson and meet him at the restaurant."

"Just make sure he takes you home."

"Oh, he *will*," she said, her tone dripping in innuendoes.

With that situation resolved, we headed home. Snow was moping around the house when we arrived. "You coming with me tonight?" I asked her.

She dragged her gaze from the ghostly book she was reading. "Yes, I suppose so."

"If you don't want to, you don't have to."

"Hey, why does she get to go, and I don't?" Cammie snapped.

"First of all, I'm trying to solve the mystery of her death. Second of all"—I gritted my teeth in frustration— "okay, there isn't a second of all, but this is her death that I'm solving. That's why she gets to go."

"And I would just get in the way?" Cammie asked sorrowfully.

My heart twisted. Dang it! No, we'd never be best friends, but I couldn't simply be mean to my sister.

I sighed and slumped onto the couch. "No, you wouldn't get in the way. That's not it."

"Then what is it?" She tapped her toe impatiently. "'Cause from where I stand, that's what it sure looks like."

How much should I tell her? Was the truth too much? Did she deserve to know? I was trying to keep her safe as well. If my sister decided that she hated me for what I could do and what I could see, so be it.

The very least that I owed her, in order to keep her safe, was the truth.

"Sit down," I said. Cammie pulled out a kitchen chair and sat at the table. I exhaled a deep sigh and sat across from her. "What I'm going to tell you...you may not believe me. In fact, if I were you, I probably wouldn't believe me at all. It's wild and crazy, and if our places were switched, I would have a hard time buying it."

"Would you just spit it out?" she said.

"Okay." Here went nothing. "There are things in Willow Lake that are a little different from other places."

"Like what?" she asked in a flat voice, one already bored with this conversation.

Oh, I understood. My sister didn't think that I would have anything to say that would make a difference. She figured I was probably going to give her some line like all the men she's dated before.

But was she about to be surprised. "When Grim talked to his friend, Al, about Pam, we learned that Pam had secrets."

"What kind?" Cammie shot up, her eyes gleaming with intrigue. "Is she some sort of crazy cat lady? Did she murder somebody and hide their body in her basement?"

"Well, you're not far off." I flexed my fingers, balling my hands. Working them helped me to concentrate. "Cammie, Willow Lake is not what you think it is."

"It ain't?" She frowned. "Seems like a quiet lake community."

"It is, but it's not." Why was I piddling around the truth? I just had to go for it. "The truth is this town is magical. It's different. The grocery store is full of werewolves. The ice cream shop sells blood ice cream for the vampires. The coffee shops are run by real witches, brewing up real potions. And I, Cammie, am a witch. Our grandmother may have been, too. I don't know. If she could see spirits, then maybe she could also cast spells. Now I know how you feel about wizards and witches, how you want to shoot us dead because no creature on God's green earth should be able to have crazy power like that. You can take this however you want. You can do to me whatever you want, but I'm telling you all of this to keep you safe."

I rose and splayed my hands on the table. I couldn't look at my sister. I didn't want to know how she was reacting to what I was telling her.

So I barreled on. "I know it all sounds crazy, and when I first arrived and realized that it was true, I fought it. I didn't want to be a witch. I didn't want to have powers. And I certainly didn't want to be stuck in a town full of other beings like werewolves. But I've gotten used to it, and if I were being perfectly honest, I kind of like it."

A soft spot in my heart opened up right then. I hadn't known how attached I'd gotten to this town until right at that moment. I didn't want to up and leave when my lease was over. I wanted to stay and see how things with Grim would go.

My gaze flicked to Cammie. She studied me with a curious expression. Since she wasn't shooting daggers from her eyes, or worse, I kept on.

"But here's the thing, Cammie, and you're going to think I'm crazy. You probably won't believe me at all, and I don't blame you. But the reason I'm telling you this is because the night when Newman was killed, Grim spotted something by the car." I paused, giving her a chance to ask what he had found. When she didn't, I said, "He found a spot that looked like it could belong to a monster."

I inhaled deeply then, ready to tackle the home stretch. Cammie still hadn't interrupted me, and I figured that was a win. "You see, Grim hunts monsters. He's a monster hunter. That's his area of expertise. Among other things," I joked.

She didn't laugh.

I cleared my throat. "The point is, there's a monster on the loose, so you can't go out alone at night. You've got to stay inside, where it's safe. And the reason I didn't want you to meet with Pam is because Pam was found with monster parts in her home. I don't know if she's dangerous. I don't know anything about her. But that's it." I threw up my hands in defeat. "That's the whole story. I know that you and I will never really be friends, and this won't help my cause in any way, but you needed to know. Do with it what you will."

Finished and exhausted from word vomiting for what felt like a rambling ten minutes, I plopped back into the chair and waited for her to speak.

Cammie licked her lips and narrowed her eyes as if going back over everything that I had said, trying to piece it together.

Finally she said, "You don't think that we'll ever be friends?"

My eyes flared wide in surprise. She didn't want to take me out back and put me out of my witchy misery? "Well," I said slowly, turning the words over in my mind before spewing them out (unlike what I'd just finished doing), "we've never really been close, and then you were really adamant about what you'd do if a wizard ever showed up on your front porch shooting lasers from his hands, so...no. I guess that I never thought we'd be close."

She nodded somberly before her eyes cut to me. "Can you shoot lasers?"

I eyed her suspiciously, unsure of where this was going. "Well, sort of. It depends. My magic is weird." I paused, expecting her to wretch in repulsion. But Cammie didn't react that way. In fact, when she simply waited patiently for me to continue, I added, "If I'm around someone for a long time, I absorb their abilities. Grim has lightning magic. He can shoot thunderbolts. So when I'm around him, yes, I can basically shoot lasers from my hands."

She studied me for a long moment. Sweat sprouted on my back and trickled down my spine. The tension was unbearable. Would Cammie grab her gun? I'd chosen to tell her for her own safety. Surely she could see that.

Or perhaps she would call the loony bin and have me thrown inside with the door locked tightly behind me.

To my shock, her face broke into a wide grin. "You can shoot lasers! That is so cool."

I paused a moment, waiting for the other shoe to drop. Did my sister know what she was saying? "Um, is that all you have to add?"

She sniffed. "No. I'm also ticked that you didn't tell me any of this earlier. Oh, I'm also mad that you think we cain't be friends. What's up with that? I thought we was doing a pretty good job on that front. We're bonding, trying to figure out who blew up Newman and his car. How can we not be friends since we've been doing all of that together? You and me, we're like Starsky and Hutch or those two women who had that one show."

"Cagney and Lacey?" I ventured.

She snapped her fingers. "That's the one. We're like those two women, fighting crime and kicking butt."

"You're not mad? You don't want to kill me?"

She flinched. "Why would I want to kill you?" I started to answer, but she stopped me with, "Oh yeah, I get it. I shot my mouth off trying to be cool and the gang and all that. But did you really think that I would hurt my own sister?"

Well yes, I did.

When I didn't answer, Cammie dropped her head into her hands. "I'm sorry that I made you feel that way." When she lifted her face, her eyes brimmed with tears. "Paige, you're my sister. No matter what sort of disagreements we've had in the past, nothing can change that. You can either love your blood and do your best to get along with one another, or you can fight and bicker. I don't want to be no bickerer."

Not sure that *bickerer* was a word, but that wasn't the point. I rose and crossed to her, wrapping my arms around her neck from behind and inhaling her rose-scented perfume.

"I'm sorry. I should've told you earlier."

She patted my hand tenderly. "I understand why you didn't."

"Well, you also can't see any of the creatures or the magic. If you witness anything, it just sort of looks like smoke to you."

"So even though you told me, I'll still be blind to it?"

"Right." I straightened and came around to face her. Our gazes locked and I felt a deep kinship with my sister. No, we didn't see eye to eye most of the time. We were incredibly different. Using a clichéd term like saying we were night and day didn't do our differences justice, but we weren't the same. We didn't have much in common. But the one thing that we did have alike was our love for one another.

My heart felt full, and I was happy. "Thank you for understanding."

She shrugged. "You're welcome. But you're right. I probably would've tried to shoot you anyway, like you said." My eyebrows arched in alarm, and she laughed. "Just kidding."

We hugged again and the doorbell rang. My gaze cut to the door. "It's Grim. Time to meet Pam."

CHAPTER 17

*C*ammie didn't come with me and Grim. Snow did, however. She sat in the back seat. I'm not sure how physics worked for ghosts. Being transparent and all, you would think that when the vehicle started moving that Snow would remain stationary, but she did not. She moved with us.

My gaze darted to the mirror, and Snow stared out the window, her eyes full of what I can only describe as a worried longing.

The ghost caught me looking into the flip-down mirror at her. She sighed. "I want to know what Pam knows, but I'm afraid."

"It's going to be fine," I murmured.

"It is very odd to be with you when you speak to ghosts," Grim told me.

I laughed. "That's not the first time I've heard that."

We wound through Willow Lake, sliding through downtown. As the houses became sparser, the trees started to encroach on the narrowing road.

My stomach knotted. Weeks of wondering what had happened to Snow could finally be answered. I glanced up into the mirror again and spotted Snow biting her bottom lip.

We would finally know the truth, and Snow could get the rest she deserved.

Grim turned down a long, winding driveway. On both sides the grass had grown to waist height. It swayed as a wind brushed over it. Beyond the meadow that was in dire need of a good bushwhacking sat a brick ranch-style home. The brick was a pale cream, and the shutters lining the windows were ebony. The wind plucked the edges of the shutters off the house, and the wooden slats flapped against the home.

A shudder ran through me. "Are you sure Pam lives here? The place looks abandoned."

Grim's jaw tightened. "She's supposed to. But no one's talked to her for years. She's a recluse."

"But she has to go into town," I argued. "She has to eat, buy groceries."

"Some people make it their job to avoid others," he said quietly, as if he'd lived this experience.

My heart tore a little for him. I squeezed his bicep, and he glanced down, his gaze telling me everything I needed to know. He'd blamed himself for his parents' death and, as his own punishment to himself, had avoided people. My eyes told him silently that he didn't have to avoid anyone. Not anymore.

He was enough.

Grim parked beside the house. The walkway was broken on the edges, the concrete crumbling into the earth. The paint on the brick exterior was peeling off in long fingers.

Basically, the whole place was charming.

Grim squeezed my hand. "Everyone ready?"

I glanced back at Snow. She nodded. "I'm ready."

Steel wind chimes hanging from the porch clanged in quite an unwelcome way as we approached. The porch itself sagged to one side, probably from the holes in the wooden boards holding it up. It was still light enough in the sky that I spotted a shadow scurrying between the holes. It was probably just a possum, I thought. But that didn't stop a deep shiver from working its way to my bones.

I gripped Grim's arm for dear life and he chuckled. He brushed his fingers over mine and murmured, "What could you be afraid of, my muse?"

"Everything," I squeaked. "This house gives me the creeps. How could anyone live here?"

"You'd be surprised the conditions that people can survive in."

I didn't want to be surprised or even imagine them. I wanted to go home. Tuck tail and run, that was me.

Good grief, if the house was this wrecked on the outside, what could it look like on the *inside?* I imagined it smelled of must and mold. Dark patches of moss probably spotted the walls and creeped over the brown shag carpet. The walls would bow in, created from moisture that was itself created by a leaky roof that didn't get fixed for a long, long time, leaving the rain ample opportunity to wreak havoc on the interior of the home.

There were also probably twenty cats. One or two of them most likely dead and buried under a mound of fur-covered blankets that hadn't seen the inside of a washing machine in years. Pam would have wondered for a while what happened to the two cats that disappeared, probably figuring that they slipped out the door one morning and got lost or taken by a hawk.

She would never suspect the truth—that they had instead been crushed by—

The doorbell sounded. I blinked and realized that we were standing on said sagging porch that, by some miracle, happened to hold my weight.

Grim's hand slipped down to his side. *He* had pushed the doorbell. Oh no. It was happening. Pam would open the door, and she would be terrifying—one cocked eye and wearing a moth-gobbled flannel shirt and some sort of gray cotton shapeless skirt and shoes with a hole in the big toe.

Her toe would be poking through, and the nail would be black and three inches lo—

"Yes?"

The door had opened and there stood Pam. She had a halo of soft white hair with a few streaks of gray in it. Her eyes were pale blue, and her skin was soft with fine creases running down the cheeks and at the corners of her eyes. Pam had a wide, kind smile. She looked like someone's grandmother, the kind of person who kept warm chocolate chip cookies available in case visitors came unexpectedly.

May I have one, please?

Pam glanced from Grim to me with a question burning in her eyes. "Yes?" she repeated. "How can I help you?"

Grim cleared his throat. "Are you Pam?"

"You've found me."

"My name's Grim and this is Paige. Paige has been searching for the truth about what happened to a woman named Snow Murry."

Pam's eyes narrowed on me. Gone was the grandmotherly appearance. Her expression became frosty in an instant.

"I don't know anyone named Snow," she told us.

Snow was beside me now. She leaned over and peered into Pam's face. Pam couldn't see her, but Snow looked Pam up and down.

"This is her," she told me. "It's Pam."

"Now if you'll excuse me." Pam took a step back and looked as if she would close the door on us.

I couldn't let that happen, so I stepped forward. "I know it's you, Pam. Snow just told me. She's a ghost and I can see her."

Pam's jaw went slack. She studied me for a long moment, her eyes full of questions. Finally she whispered, "She's out of the book, then?"

I nodded. "Yes, she is."

"And the book?" Pam brought trembling fingers to her mouth. "Where is it?"

Grim shook his head. "We don't know. It's been stolen."

Pam took my sleeve in one of her gnarled hands. "Come inside. Quickly. There's much to discuss."

You know how I'd expected mold to be growing up the walls in Pam's house? Well, it turned out that the facade was all an illusion—a very good one.

The interior of the home was perfect. The floors didn't sag, and there was no vegetation invading the place that I could see. Instead delicate lace doilies draped antique tables that were topped with porcelain figurines. There was a curio cabinet filled with cherubic statues, and Pam's dinner table sat six and each place setting was made.

In all, the home was tidy and well-kept.

Grim took one look around and smirked. "You don't want anyone to bother you."

Pam slipped a chain over a lock and tugged on the doorknob to make sure it was secured tight. "I have enemies."

"Would that include half of town?" I asked.

Pam chuckled. "No, I don't much worry about them. They've had their eyeballs filled with enough horror at my house to keep me safe from them. They won't be coming back here anytime soon."

I exchanged a concerned look with Grim. "What do you mean?"

"Sit," she instructed us, pointing to two love seats facing each other just inside the door. "Would you like something to drink? Tea? Coffee?"

"Whatever's easiest," I told her.

Pam shuffled off into the kitchen, which was just one room over. She spoke to us while she put together a snack. Silverware clanged as she spoke. "I pulled a good trick on them years ago. Several had been snooping around. I've always kept my house looking bad, for good reason, so that no one thinks much about me. I'd learned my lesson with that before. Makes me too easy to find."

I shot Grim a what-in-the-world-is-she-talking-about look, and he returned it with, *Just go with it.*

I sank back onto the couch. Okay, I would just go with it. Meanwhile, Snow was studying a table full of pictures, running her fingers over the faces of the people.

Pam emerged from the kitchen holding a tray of brownies and coffee. Grim rose and helped her settle it on the table between the couches.

"Now then." Pam sat with a huff. "Tell me how you'd like your coffee."

She served us and then continued on with her story. "I knew the people out here were upset with the way I'd let the house go." Pam chuckled, laughing at the inside joke that she had with herself. "But anyway, to really give them something to talk about, I placed what looked like monster body parts everywhere. Just to scare them, you know?"

Sounded like a great joke to me—let people think they had a potential serial killer as a neighbor.

Perhaps that *wasn't* the best joke to play on folks.

"They were all in an uproar about it." Pam handed me a cup of coffee. "But there wasn't anything they could do. They weren't people. They weren't even real. By the time the police arrived, I had them all gone. But I like the suspicion that lingers about me. Keeps my business private and keeps people from asking too many questions." Her gaze latched on to me and then Grim. "But I have the feeling that you're going to ask me a lot of questions. More than I've answered in a long time."

Grim nodded to me and I sat up. "I moved into a cabin rental for the summer. On the first day that I arrived, I found a book. When I was putting it away, it fell on my head and knocked me out. When that happened, it released Snow Murry. I know this sounds crazy, but after being hit on the head, I was able to see ghosts. Snow was the first ghost that I met. She told me that she'd been trapped in that book since the nineties. She didn't know what had happened to her. She still can't remember. But she recalled your name, said you were her neighbor. The book was called—"

"*A Study in the Paranormal* by Heronomous Spell," Pam interrupted.

"Yes." Surprise coated my voice. "That was it. Tell me how you know."

Pam took a luxuriously long sip from her coffee and settled the cup on the table. Then she dabbed a napkin to each corner of her mouth and said to me, her eyes sparkling with intrigue, "I know the title of that book because it was mine."

"It was?" I was shocked. I could not believe what I was hearing. "The book belonged to you?"

"It sure did." Pam leaned forward conspiratorially. Her eyes still glimmered when she added, "And I'm the person who trapped Snow in it."

CHAPTER 18

Snow shot over to us. "She did what? She trapped me? Why?" Her features twisted in fury. "Why, I'll trap *her* in that book. Once I find it, that is. How could Pam do that to me?"

Pam's gaze flickered around. "Is Snow here?"

"Yes," I told her.

"I'm sure she's angry."

"That's an understatement."

She nodded in understanding. It was Grim who spoke next. "You have some explaining to do. By placing Snow in the book, you ended her life."

"I know." Pam dropped her head into her hands. "It wasn't on purpose—the ending part. Snow"—her eyes roamed the room— "you have to believe me."

Snow folded her arms. Ghostly fingernails dug into her naked biceps. "I don't believe anything right now." Her gaze flicked to me. "Ask her why she did it."

"Snow wants to know why."

Pam lifted her face and nodded. "Of course she does. She has every right to."

I frowned. "You don't seem surprised by that."

"What? That she can't remember?"

"Yes," I said.

Pam ran her fingers over her hair. "I'm not surprised because before I dropped Snow into the book, I stole some of her memories."

"Why?" Snow snarled.

Though Pam couldn't hear her, she answered the question, as it was the most logical thing to do next. "You see, Snow's husband wasn't a good man. He was terrible. He would sometimes come home and those two would get into awful fights. I could hear them from next door. Snow would end up crying. One day she confided to me that her husband was a violent man. She was worried about how far his violence would go. I told her that if she ever needed my help, that I was just next door. I would do anything for her. Snow and I were friends, you see."

"We were," Snow murmured quietly.

Pam wrung her hands with worry. "Then one day Snow appeared at my door. She said that he'd hurt her. She had a bruise on her arm. She begged me to take her in. That he was looking for her, but she'd run out of the house. He would search for her, she told me. Please, I remember her saying. Please hide me."

Pam paused for a moment, and I knew what she was going to say next. Grim seemed to know as well. He squeezed my hand, offering comfort.

"I had the book," Pam told us. "It was in my possession and had been for years. I was its keeper. I knew that things that went into it could come out again. If Snow's husband was as angry as she said, he would search my house for her. I realized that," she said sharply, her eyes alight with anger. "I hid her in the only place that I knew he'd never look—the book."

Pam sighed, deflating onto the couch. "If I could go back and change things, I would. I would take it back. Instead I would have hidden Snow in the basement or a bathroom. Yes, he might've found her. But I could have called the police and gotten her to safety. But instead I put her in the book, and no, her husband didn't find her."

There was a long pause, and I sensed that for some reason Pam didn't want to go on. But before I could push her, Grim did.

"Why didn't you release her immediately?"

Pam shook her head. "I should have, but I was worried that he'd come back. And maybe, if I'd pulled her from the book right then, she could've been saved. But I left her in and what happened next was a shock even to me."

I picked at the edge of my fingernail. "What was that?"

"The book disappeared."

I sucked air. It was the same thing that had happened to me. "When?"

"That very night," she told us. "I'd been the keeper of it for years, only using the book when I found a monster nearby. It was started by Heronomous Spell, but then the book was passed on from keeper to keeper. We were to capture creatures in it to keep people safe. There were detailed instructions inside the book flap, describing our job. But I hadn't used the book in years. There hadn't been anything to capture. I thought it was safe to place Snow inside. But I went out for a bit, and when I returned, the book was gone."

"Gone?" I whispered.

Pam nodded. "Every so often it leaves the person in charge of it as it searches for a new keeper. It appeared to me years ago, and I kept it safe. Believe me," she said, her voice laced with regret, "if I'd known that Snow was going to wind up trapped and dead in that book, I never would've stowed her inside, not even for a moment."

Grim frowned at me, trouble brewing in his eyes. "That sounds similar to what happened to you."

Pam's gaze flicked to me. "What does that mean?"

"The book vanished right after it landed on my head and spit out Snow."

"Thanks," Snow said sarcastically.

"So maybe 'spit out' wasn't the right phrase."

"No, it *was*. That was what happened. I just hate to think about it that way."

I understood completely. But before I could find time to ponder her words, Pam shot over to me and took my hands. "Snow? Where is she?"

I pointed just to the left of Pam. "She's right there."

Pam turned and her eyes didn't quite settle on Snow, but her gaze was near her. "Snow, I'm so sorry for what happened to you. I searched for the book after it left me. I searched high and low but couldn't find it. If I had, I would've taken you out before the book's power had time to make you a permanent fixture in it."

"It's okay," Snow said, wiping a faint tear from her eyelash. "It all happened for a reason."

But I was consumed with another thought. "The book found a new keeper. But whoever it is, they've let a monster out before."

Pam sucked air. "You're kidding."

"I wish we were," Grim said in a voice sharpened with anger. "We've been searching for the book but haven't found any sign of it."

"I can't help you there," Pam told us sadly. "Once it's found a keeper, we can't locate it."

"Whoever owned the cabin before Patricia bought it was the previous keeper," I murmured, trying to slide puzzle pieces together.

"It seems like. But now there's a new one." Grim scrubbed a hand down his cheek and said to Pam, "So were you a hunter?"

"More someone who kept things as they were. I wasn't like you," she said, her gaze washing up and down him. "I'm not going to chase down and capture a creature."

I thumbed toward Grim. "How do you know what he is?"

Pam laughed. "You might be a witch, but you have a lot to learn about recognizing a hunter."

"She's new," Grim explained.

"Oh, I see." Pam folded her hands in her lap and appraised me. "I know this man is a hunter by the way he walks, the way he looks at everything with suspicion in his eyes."

I frowned. Wasn't that Grim's normal look? Suspicion with a touch of frustration? "I don't get it."

"Perhaps it's because I was one of the keepers," Pam said a little too wistfully for my taste. Who wanted to be in charge of a book loaded with monstrous drawings? "I got used to seeing the creatures. I admired their deadly beauty."

"You wouldn't have admired the *aghash* with its one thousand tentacles and eyes," I told her firmly.

She shrugged. "Perhaps not. But it was interesting. And that's one reason why I wanted to keep people away from me. Even though I wasn't in charge of the book anymore, I didn't know how safe I really was. Could I be tracked by someone looking to have the book themselves? That's what I feared. It's why the house looks rotten on the outside, and all that. I'm sure you noticed how shabby the exterior is." I nodded and she clasped her hands. "Ah, well. What's done is done. I can't go back. Hopefully Snow, you will forgive me?"

Snow nodded. "I forgive you."

I told Pam and a small tear spilled from her eye. "That's good to know."

The conversation appeared to be wrapping up, so I started to rise but Grim's voice stopped me. "Have you studied monsters a lot?"

Pam's head whipped in his direction. "Why?" she asked, her voice thick with worry.

"I found something at a crime scene the other day. A dark, oily spot."

Her brows lifted in surprise. "Darkling sign?"

"Yes. Here."

He pulled a picture up on his phone and handed it to her. Pam studied it for a moment and then rose, pressing a finger to her lips. She handed the phone back to Grim before crossing the room to her bookcase.

"I don't have a lot of titles on monsters, not like I'm sure you have." She glanced over her shoulder and gave Grim a pointed look, as if waiting for him to confirm her suspicion.

"I have many," he told her.

She nodded in approval and pinned her focus back on the case. She ran her finger along the leather spines of gold-lettered books as she talked.

"That looks like darkling sign, but you're not convinced, which is why you showed the picture to me. I saw it, and it does very clearly appear to be what you're saying, but I noticed something else."

"The yellow grass."

She smiled at him. "Right. The yellow grass."

What were they talking about? "Can I see?"

Grim handed me the phone, and my gaze skimmed the picture. It was dark, but his flash had caught a greasy mark on the earth. There was yellow grass around the spot, so I wasn't sure what they were talking about until I saw it.

In the very center of the oily substance sat a small piece of grass. Everything to the edges of the dark blotch was ebony. There was no color. But then why was there one small fragment of grass in the very center with a different hue?

"Do you think someone kicked it into the spot when they were walking? Or the explosion caused it to happen?" I asked, thinking those were perfectly logical explanations for what we were looking at.

But Grim shook his head. "I don't think so. It doesn't look like any other grass blades around. It's shaped differently."

"Exactly," Pam replied, poking the air for added effect. "It's not made of the same sort of grass as what's surrounding it. Now, where is that book? Ah, here it is."

It was slim and looked more like a journal than an actual printing. "What's that?"

"This is the writings of a wizard from long ago." Pam's fingers curled around a pair of reading glasses that sat on a table. "I don't look at it often, and I don't know how much help it will actually be to you, but it may offer some insight."

What were they talking about? "Grim already knows how to fight darklings."

"Which would be very helpful if you were actually *dealing* with a darkling," she said.

My gaze snapped to Grim. He sat, eyes on Pam, his jaw jumping in frustration. He suspected that there was more to the monster at the lake than what he'd originally told me. I was almost hurt that he hadn't revealed his suspicions to me before.

"Now where is that entry?" Pam flipped through the thin pages. Even from my spot on the couch across from her, I could see the light piercing the paper. Those pages were old, older than anything I'd looked on before.

After a moment she jabbed the page with her finger. "Here's the entry I was looking for. I'll read." She cleared her throat. "'The creature leaves a strand of itself often behind it, after it's worked evil. The evil can be of varying degrees—from death of an animal to that of a child. It can also be destruction in the form of a house burning or even trees in a forest catching fire. I have witnessed both, and behind both were the markings that could easily have been misinterpreted to be that of a darkling.'" Pam's gaze cut to Grim. "Just like you thought."

"Who wrote this?" he asked.

"An old wizard—Langferous Lollow. I happened to be lucky enough to find this copy at a witch and wizard bookstore."

Grim fingers clenched and unclenched. "I haven't heard of him."

"That's because he wasn't a hunter, just a wizard observing things. Let me keep going." She waited for Grim's approval and when he nodded, Pam dived right back in. "'But this marking is different. It has the yellow of its flesh that it leaves behind, as if losing a piece of itself. I never wanted to meet the creature alone, though that did happen one afternoon. I sat high in a tree, watching and waiting to see what was killing the cattle of a farmer. The thing approached with a lumbering gait and death in its eyes. Nothing in its path was of any consequence. It paid no more attention to a passing bee than it did a raging bull. Nothing scared the creature. In my haste I drew this picture of it before I attacked.

"'No lightning bolt that I cast, nor fire caused any harm to the thing. In the end I had to flee and prayed to leave unharmed. The creature cannot be killed. I have lived to tell of the beast. But know that no mere mortal can defeat the thing, and I only barely escaped with my life.'"

Pam stopped and her eyes scanned the page. When she didn't speak, Grim said, "Is that it?"

"There is a picture."

"Let me see it."

Pam lifted the book for us, and I gasped. I thought that I'd see some monster with dark, shaggy hair, maybe a cyclops. But I didn't expect what I saw.

It was light yellow, and its skin looked to have been made from a corn husk. The limbs were long, with roping muscles, and at its head rose a crown of feathery husks. The creature looked strong enough to take down an elephant with one swing. But the eyes—those were the scariest—inky black and full of death, just as the wizard had described. I shuddered just looking at it.

Pam shook her head sadly. "What we've got on our hands isn't a darkling, something you can destroy, but a withering, the one creature that no man has ever defeated and lived to tell about it."

CHAPTER 19

he next morning it took everything I had to force thoughts of the withering from my mind.

So it wasn't a darkling after all. It was a withering that was on the loose. And how had I not seen it the night that Newman died? Had it been at the scene before we arrived? Surely I would have noticed a creature sneak up to Newman's car while we were doing the trade-off with the duffel bag of money.

Wouldn't I?

Grim had seemed rattled over the entire thing. He'd confessed before to not knowing much about witherings. No one did because few lived to tell after they'd encountered one. It also didn't aid in my confidence that the wizard who'd written in the journal that Pam had read confessed that he'd tried to kill the creature with fire and that hadn't worked.

If fire couldn't kill it, what could?

Perhaps Pam was wrong. Maybe what we were dealing with wasn't a withering after all.

I lay in bed the next morning fighting off a chill that had settled into my bones at the mere thought of a withering. With any luck, I would never have to see such a creature. Most likely there was nothing for me to worry about.

I pushed myself out of bed and heard voices coming from the living room. I slid my arms into a robe and opened the door to find Abraham with a pad and pencil in his hand, talking to Cammie.

"Yep, I can get you some tuna fish," he said. "Whatever else you need. Do you need eggs?"

"No thanks." My sister opened the fridge. "We could use some milk. Maybe some creamer." Her gaze slid to me and she grinned. "Abe here is taking up a grocery list. You want some cream?"

"I can go into town myself and get what we need. I hate to make Abe do so much work."

"It's okay." He scratched something onto his pad. "I'm happy to go. Keeps me busy. Makes me tired so that I sleep at night."

I found it strange that a kid like him had a hard time sleeping. "You don't sleep well?"

He shook his head. "Nah, I have a lot on my mind. It keeps me up."

"I see." But I didn't.

I moved to the coffee maker and grabbed a mug sitting beside it. The carafe was full of coffee. Cammie had done me a solid by making it before I woke. I poured a cup and took a long sip while Abraham continued to speak.

"Yeah, you know. This is a strange town and all. I have a lot of responsibility. Not just to y'all, but also..."

"But also, to what?" I asked.

He shook his head. "Never mind. Listen, ladies, is there anything else that I can get you?" He rattled off the list that he and Cammie had worked on. "Is there one more thing you need?"

"Not that I can think of," Cammie told him.

"Great. I'll get this to you later today. Bye, now."

As soon as Abraham left, I turned to Cammie. "Did you call him?"

"No, he came on his own." She tied her hair back in a ponytail. "So, what're we going to do today? We going to do any more fishing?"

"I've got a book to finish." She made a face that made my heart squeeze. "I'm sorry. I really am, but I've got to get it done. I'm under contract, a contract that I'm grateful to have."

Cammie nodded. "That's fine. I was going to track down that Herman fellow anyway, see what he knew about Newman's death."

Alarm bells blared in the back of my head. "Cammie, I'm not sure that's a good idea."

"Why not?"

"Well…" I sipped from my coffee, hoping it would give me a bit of caffeinated courage. "You know how I told you that there are weird things in this town?"

She quirked a perfectly plucked brow. "Yes?"

I explained what we had learned about the withering and finished with, "So you've got to be careful. If one of Newman's assassin friends is in cahoots with a creature like that, they would be extremely dangerous."

She seemed to weigh that for a minute before replying. "I'll take my chances." Cammie slung her purse over her shoulder. "Don't worry. You know that I'm packing heat. I'll be just fine."

I rolled my eyes. "Oh Lord." I did not want my sister running around Willow Lake with a handgun and a point to make. "Let me get dressed and I'll go with you to do…whatever it is you plan on."

I showered and dressed, looking around the cabin for Snow, who was not anywhere to be seen. She hadn't said much after Pam confessed to why she'd stuck Snow in the book, and I wondered what, exactly, was on her mind.

After dressing, I promised myself that I would work on the book when we returned. But for now I had to keep Cammie from doing anything stupid, like shooting up downtown.

We headed out.

My eyelids were peeled back wide as I drove us through the streets. I watched the scenery obsessively, worried that the withering would jump out at us at any moment. But there were no monsters that morning, just a warm sun casting golden light across the town and a crisp breeze that signaled the beginning of fall and the end of summer.

"Where do you think we'll find Herman?" I asked.

Cammie clicked her tongue. "Where do you think bookworms hang out?"

I thought about it, and we both said at the same time, "The library."

The Willow Lake Public Library was a red brick building with large sliding glass doors and big windows that let in lots of light.

The head librarian, Vanessa, greeted us upon arrival. She was a vampire, but I'd never gotten the feeling that she had any interest in biting my neck, which was a good thing.

"So glad that we ran into you," I cooed. "Have you seen a young man with his nose in a book?"

Vanessa tossed her head back and laughed lightly. "This is a library. Everyone here has their nose in a book."

Good point. "We'll just look around then."

And so we did. Cammie and I perused the aisles, but I didn't see hide nor hair of Herman. Maybe he'd left. But Pippa and Stanislav had both said that they were all staying in Willow Lake until the murderer was found. They wanted to know what happened to Newman as much as we did.

Cammie approached me, looking deflated. "I guess he ain't here. Let's keep looking."

We headed outside and walked down the main drag, peering into the store windows to see if maybe Herman was inside one of the shops.

The door to the Witch's Brew coffee shop opened and out came Stanislav. He held the door for the person behind him and out slinked Pippa. She stopped and ran her hands down the hem of her oversize T-shirt, straightening it. When she looked up, Stanislav leaned over and kissed her.

My chest tightened.

Cammie clutched my shoulder. "Did you just see what I just saw?"

"Mr. Married kissing Pippa? I sure did."

"What in the world is that all about?"

"I have no idea."

"Quick." Cammie pulled me behind a potted bush. "Let's follow them."

"Let's what?"

"Follow them. You know, we can really relive being Cagney and Lacey."

"I don't want to be Cagney and Lacey."

She tugged my shirt. "Sure you do. Come on."

I was about to say no when the two lovebirds stopped walking as they waited for a light to turn. They faced one another and Stanislav kissed Pippa again. Then he brushed a hair from her face.

He had pointed us in Pippa's direction, saying that she had more reason to want to kill Newman than he did. And of course, he'd never mentioned that they were in a relationship—or affair, as it was. If I didn't follow them, it would be highly irresponsible of me.

Because it was more than possible that Pippa and Stanislav were in this whole thing together.

"Okay," I grudgingly admitted. "Let's follow them."

We practically tiptoed down the street, ducking behind bushes and turning to face windows whenever it seemed like Stanislav or Pippa was about to turn around.

"It's safe to come out now," Cammie told me after I'd face-planted into the windows of a local restaurant.

My gaze roved the street, but I didn't see the lovers. "Where'd they go?"

"Into that store," she told me, pointing to a children's clothing boutique.

That was a strange place for the lovers to have disappeared into. But that didn't stop me from saying, "Let's check it out."

There was just one problem—we'd already ambushed Pippa in a store. It would seem way *more* than coincidental if we did so again. And they wouldn't talk, that was for sure. So just as Cammie was reaching for the door handle, I grabbed her.

"Let's hold on a moment."

"Hold on for what?"

The voice had sounded behind me, sending chills dancing all the way down my spine. I turned to see Grim standing there, wearing a black button-down shirt and pants. His sleeves were rolled up, revealing his muscular forearms—muscles that he probably built fighting that stupid wooden structure that tried to kill me.

"Oh, Grim. Hey."

He eyed me with what I like to call *amused suspicion*. "Hey, yourself," he said in a low growl, sending tingles shimmering all over my body again. "What's going on?"

Cammie pointed to the shop. "Well, we are about to ambush two people who have lied to us. We're going in there to find out if they killed Newman."

Grim quirked a brow. "Is that so?"

"Yes," I replied, suddenly feeling quite defensive. "We are. In fact," I added, suddenly remembering about the oily stain on Pippa's purse (how had I forgotten that?), "I think the woman may know something about our little withering problem."

Grim's face hardened to steel. His eyes became chips of burnt emeralds. "What do you mean?"

Knowing that time was ticking away, I quickly explained what I'd seen on the bottom of Pippa's purse. "It looked like oil," I said. "I'm sorry that I forgot to mention it before. I shouldn't have. It's just that we've been so busy with Snow and everything."

Grim looked past us, into the store. "I'll go talk to her."

"Great! We're coming with you," Cammie announced. Grim turned to her, his expression screaming that he was about to tell her no, when Cammie added, "I gotta know why Newman was killed. You ain't gonna stop me, so don't even try."

He sighed and said to me, "There isn't a way to convince her otherwise, is there?"

I shook my head. "I'm afraid not. She's always this headstrong."

His lips curled into a seductive smile. "Stubbornness must run in your family."

My cheeks immediately heated, and right then and there I wanted to be alone with Grim. But instead of yanking him into my car and having my way with him, I murmured, "I suppose it does."

He took hold of the handle and opened the glass door. At the same time, a small metal ball shot out of the shop. I stared at it, wondering where it had come from. But before I was able to verbalize the question, the top of the ball opened with a *snick* and gas poured out of it.

"Quick! Move," Grim commanded, pushing me and Cammie out of the way.

Before I could get far, the gas reached my nose. It was an acrid, sulfuric smell—overwhelming is the smallest way to describe it.

I found myself overcome with the fumes, and the next thing I knew, my legs were folding even though I didn't mean for them to, and I was falling to the ground.

CHAPTER 20

*W*hen I came to, Grim was kneeling over me. My head felt like a sledgehammer had been taken to it, and my legs were weak.

Grim's hand cradled my head. "Are you okay?"

I tried to answer, but instead of words coming from my mouth, a cough ejected. After a moment I managed to croak, "Yes, I'm fine. What happened?"

His gaze cut up to where Pippa and Stanislav were standing. "That's what happened," he growled.

Pippa shrugged. "I thought our lives were in danger. We were being followed."

"By two women," Cammie shot out.

Stanislav gave Cammie a sympathetic look. "We've been followed before. I think my wife is on to us."

"You think?" she snapped. "Y'all were kissing on the street. If she suspected anything, she wouldn't have to look too far into it. Y'all are practically showing off."

Pippa's face wrinkled in worry. "It's one reason why we're staying in town. So that we can be together."

Stanislav reached for her, and Pippa slid into his side. He held her tight, and my stomach clenched. I knew what they had was real, like how I felt about Grim. My gaze flashed to him, and he scowled.

Clearly Grim was not thinking the same thing.

"You have oil on the bottom of your purse," Grim pointed out to Pippa.

She sighed and tipped it to get a better view. "I know. My five-hundred-dollar purse is ruined. I laid it down at a store and accidentally put it on top of carpet that was soaked with this gross stuff." She wiped at it, but the stain remained. "It won't come off."

"I was there," Stanislav said. "What she says is true."

"May I see it?"

"Sure, but I don't get what the big deal is." Pippa flipped her dark hair over one shoulder. Her thick locks curtained one side of her face, hiding one of her eyes. The other eye studied Grim quizzically. "Is there something here that I'm missing?"

Grim ran his hand down the stain and then sniffed the leather.

Pippa's eyes darted to Stanislav. "I think it's fuel."

Grim nodded and handed the purse back to her.

"The stain won't come out." She gave us a bored stare. "Is that all you wanted? Just to know what was on the bottom of my purse?"

"The explosion," Grim said. "Where were you when it happened?"

Pippa glanced at Stanislav and his gaze dropped. His cheeks glowed red, and I knew exactly *what* they had been doing, but I didn't know where.

"We walked off," the knife wielder explained. "We were given a moment to be together, so we took it."

"It's hard to find those," Pippa added.

Grim continued. "Did you see if anyone approached the vehicle?"

Prickles slithered down my spine. So Grim *did* think that it was possible that whoever caused the vehicle to explode may have tampered with the engine *after* Newman parked his car.

Stanislav and Pippa exchanged a look. It was Stanislav who answered. "We didn't. We weren't in the right, um, place to see anything."

"What about the other man?" Cammie snapped. "Where was he? Did y'all see him?"

"Herman?" Pippa shook her head, making her silky locks sway back and forth. "I didn't see him. But I don't pay any attention to him. Not because I don't think he's talented. He is. Very much so. And dangerous, just like us. As you witnessed."

"Yes, being knocked out by a fart has been the pinnacle of my existence," I said sarcastically. "Listen, do you know where to find Herman?"

Pippa pulled a pad of paper from her purse and wrote down some information. "He's staying at the same place we are. Newman put us up there."

She ripped off a page and handed the sheet to me. On it she'd written the name of a motel outside of town. I'd driven past it but had never been inside. It was the sort of place that was shaped in a U and its vacancy sign was always lit up. It also offered cable and telephones.

So yep, the place was ancient.

I thanked her and they walked off, leaving the three of us alone. "Well," Cammie said, tapping her watch, "Abraham should be back with the food. I'd better get home to let him in."

"Don't you want to question Herman?" I asked.

Cammie sucked her teeth. "I'm really hungry, is what I am. Eat first, then I'll be able to think better. Besides, that stink bomb made me nauseous. I need to lay down."

Grim turned to me. "If you want to stay out, I can drive you home in a while."

"I think I'll do that."

We said goodbye and I followed Grim to his car. As soon as we got inside, he smiled at me. "How about I cook you some lunch? I've got chicken breasts thawing and was going to cook them up with a salad."

"Sounds ridiculously healthy," I told him with a teasing smirk.

"Sounds like I'm trying to stay alive so that I can spend time with you."

A blush heated my cheeks. He was staring at me, and I suddenly felt as if the entire focus of the world was on me. I raked my fingers through my hair and murmured that I would love to eat some chicken.

When we reached his house, Savage gave my hand a big lick and then he sat with me on the couch while Grim started cooking.

"How's Snow?" he asked.

"I haven't seen her," I admitted. "I'm worried that she crossed over without me knowing. I didn't even get a chance to say goodbye."

He paused what he was doing and glanced over. "If she did cross, you should have some peace in that."

"I should, but I don't."

"Tell me," he said, his eyes narrowing.

The smell of cooking chicken and spices filled the house. I plucked a nut from a bowl lying on the coffee table and made my way to the kitchen island, where I draped my arms across the granite top.

"Well, I don't feel great about it because I don't know how she feels. Is she angry at Pam? Is she sad about all the living she missed out on? Oh boy, does that smell amazing."

A delicious smile quirked his lips. "I hope it tastes as great, too."

"I'm sure it will. I can't wait to have some and then get back out there and find out what happened to Newman." I paused. "Do you think the withering came from the book?"

Grim's shoulders tightened as if he was angry. "I don't want you to worry about the withering."

I laughed because that was ridiculous. "How could I not be concerned with it? It's out there and could potentially kill someone else."

He glanced over his shoulder, giving me a great view of his beautiful face in profile—hard jaw, straight nose, piercing eyes—completely swoonworthy. "What we're dealing with is dangerous. I want you to leave it alone."

Was he growling now? I frowned. "But I've come this far. I'm not leaving it alone. I don't care what you say. If it's dangerous, I want it gone."

At that, Grim turned around and pinned his searing gaze on me. My breath caught in my throat from the intensity burning from his eyes.

"Paige, don't be stubborn."

I scoffed. "I'm not being stubborn. I'm trying to get to the bottom of this mystery. Someone killed Newman. There was sign of a withering left at the crime scene. Mostly those two things are connected. If I don't search, Cammie will. She also wants to know who did it."

"And I said it's dangerous."

What was dangerous was the look in Grim's eyes. Was he being a big alpha male because he wanted to protect me? "I'm a big girl. I can take care of myself."

"Not around this thing, you can't." He shook his head and exhaled a deep breath. "For once, can you listen to me? I might know what I'm talking about."

"I listen to you," I stammered.

He cocked his head, clearly indicating that complying was not my best characteristic. "No, you don't. In fact, you often do the opposite. But this creature that we're dealing with is deadly."

"So are all of them," I replied, folding my arms defiantly. "I have magic."

His jaw was so tight the muscle was jumping now. "But magic won't save you. Please," he whispered.

It was the *please* that got me. He was big. He was grouchy and grim, obviously, but when he said *please*, I studied him. A deep probing pain was buried in his eyes. He gazed at me with sorrow, and I realized that what he felt for me ran deeper than what he had let on.

I took a step toward him, closing the distance between us, and pressed my palm to his cheek. He turned to my hand and closed his eyes.

"I'm sorry," I murmured. "I didn't mean to fight. I'll listen to you."

"My muse," he said in a low voice.

A shiver wound around my spine at the sound of my nickname on his lips. His eyes opened and our gazes locked. He kissed me then, and I melted into him. The kiss started slowly, his lips apologizing for being so terse and mine telling him that it was okay, I was a bit headstrong and often didn't listen to people—namely him.

"Paige," he murmured. "Tell me your secrets."

"Only if you tell me yours first," I whispered.

He chuckled and his breath tickled my neck. "I've told you mine."

I sighed and untangled myself from him, returning to sit at the counter. "For a long time after everything happened with Walter, I felt like a failure."

His jaw tightened. "Why?"

"I don't know. Because I had a failed marriage and I'd married a peeping Tom. I might as well have worn a sign that read, 'I make poor life choices.'"

"No, *he* made poor life choices," Grim said sharply. "You didn't do anything wrong. You were trying to make a life for the two of you— writing books. And he was a leech, draining you for everything that you had. Paige"—he tipped my chin until our gazes locked— "you deserve more, and I can only hope that I never let you down."

My heart grew a little bit in that moment. Pure joy swelled within me, and I rose from my seat and walked around the counter that Grim had been leaning over. I wrapped my arms around his waist, and he held me close.

There are some moments when words don't need to be spoken, when the only language you need is what your body gives and receives. This was that moment. I put all my heart into that hug, and his body responded by taking and giving it all back, and then some.

The kisses that he placed at the top of my head slowly drifted down to my neck. My hands ran over his chest, and I unabashedly felt every muscle, even smiled as his stomach quivered from my touch.

I won't go into details here, but Grim picked me up and took me into the bedroom. He emerged when the fire alarm sounded. Grim raced into the kitchen, and it was then that I caught a whiff of burnt chicken.

He appeared at the doorway holding a smoldering skillet plus an embarrassed grin on his face. "I think our lunch is ruined."

I pulled sheets around me tightly and laughed. "That's okay. Why don't we pick up where we left off and we can grab something to go later."

He chuckled. "Sounds good to me."

He left the skillet in the kitchen and came back to the bedroom, where we picked up exactly where we had left off. Even though I was having the time of my life, I couldn't help but think in the back of my mind that the withering was out there somewhere, and it was possible that Herman held the answers.

Soon as we could, we needed to find Herman and discover what he knew.

CHAPTER 21

I was on cloud nine the rest of the day. So was Grim. There was a lot of smiling between us, and my heart was so full, I knew that it couldn't get any bigger.

And Grim wasn't even his usual grumpy self. He tucked stray hairs behind my ear, made me tall glasses of ice water and he even rubbed my back.

I hadn't even asked him to.

My heart hadn't felt so happy in years. We hit a drive-through chicken restaurant after our lunch had gotten burned, and we sat in the car outside of the motel eating.

"This is a great sandwich," I told him.

Grim thumbed a crumb from my mouth. "I knew you'd like it."

"You really know how to treat a girl," I joked. "Chicken and drive-throughs."

He laughed. "Soon as we get rid of this withering, we'll go on a real date."

I quirked a brow. "Do tell."

Grim smiled shyly. I swear his cheeks tinged pink. "I shouldn't be saying this in a car."

"Why? Is it going to explode?"

He shot me a scathing look. "No, what I mean is, I haven't met anyone like you."

A tingle danced down my spine all the way to my toes. "Oh?"

"I haven't. You've brought laughter into my life, something that I haven't experienced in a long time."

He opened his hand, and I dropped my own into it. He squeezed his fingers around mine. "I haven't felt anything like this in a long, long time."

Emotion bubbled up in my chest, threatening to overwhelm me. If this was infatuation, it was an ocean of it, the emotions so strong that they threatened to overcome me.

I managed a weak smile. "I haven't felt this way in a long time, either."

We stayed like that a moment before I felt Grim stiffen. "Is that him?"

My gaze cut to the windshield. Walking from the parking lot toward one of the rooms was Herman, nose deep in a book.

"That's him," I said.

"Let's see what he has to say."

We exited the car, and I followed Grim to the room that Herman had just disappeared into. He gave a hard knock, and a voice from inside called, "Just a minute."

About a minute later the door opened, and Herman stood there, nose in a book. Sheesh. Didn't this guy ever look at the world around him? Books were great, but you had to live life every once in a while.

"Yes?" he said.

"My name is Grim."

"Okay."

Grim's neck tightened in irritation. "I wanted to talk to you about the death of a man named Newman."

"Okay," Herman repeated.

"Do you have a minute?"

"Sure."

"Can you get your nose out of that book?" Grim growled.

Herman slowly lowered the book. He had, for lack of a better word, a *bookish* face. His nose was shaped like a triangle, large and hooked on the end. His hair looked as if it had been cut with a bowl sitting atop it.

His tortoiseshell-framed glasses were perfectly large circles that magnified his eyes, making them appear twice as large as they were.

"What would you like to talk about?" he asked.

"Can we come inside?"

"Do you have a badge?" Herman said, his gaze dancing over Grim in suspicion.

"No, and I don't need one, because I have a feeling you may know about a monster that's loose in this town."

Herman's eyes widened. His gaze cut to both sides of us, and he grabbed Grim by the shirt and dragged him inside. "Quiet. No one can know."

Confused but totally curious, I followed Herman into the room. He shut the motel door behind him and pointed to the edge of the bed.

"That's the best I can offer by way of a couch. Mind the books."

Stacked two feet high were piles of books that covered the bed except for a rectangle at the very edge. "You traveled with all of these?" I asked.

Herman inhaled deeply. "Reading is good for the soul."

I supposed it was, but sleeping was, too.

Grim sat and I followed suit. He spoke. "What do you know about the monster?"

"Finally, someone else knows about it." Herman sat in the single chair in the room and dropped his face into his hands. "I thought I was seeing things."

Grim and I exchanged a curious look. "Tell us what happened," he said.

Herman pulled his trembling hands away from his face. "Newman hired me to make sure that this woman, Cammie, wouldn't do anything funny when he tried to recover some money she'd stolen from him."

"My sister," I told him. "Cammie is my sister."

His eyes flared with surprise. "She is?"

I scoffed, unable to believe this guy's attitude. "You saw us the day that Newman confronted her in the restaurant."

He shrugged. "I was reading. I listen to most conversations."

I had no comment for that.

Grim prodded him. "Then what happened?"

"Right." Herman ran his hands up and down his thighs as if drying nervous sweat from them. "I was supposed to show up at the rendezvous point, which I did, along with two other people." His eyes cut to Grim. "Have you talked to them? Did they see it, too?"

Grim shook his head. "As far as I know, they haven't."

Herman exhaled a gusty sigh. "I wish that I hadn't. But anyway, we were in the woods after Newman had called us out. I figured the woman would hand over the cash, and she did. So I was ready to leave. I turned to go, and that's when I saw it."

"Saw what?" I asked, my own palms beginning to sprout with sweat. I quickly dried them on my pants and held my breath, waiting for Herman's answer.

He lifted his hands above his head and flexed his fingers like claws. "This *thing* walked through the forest, heading straight for Newman's car."

Grim leaned forward, interest clearly piqued. "Can you describe it?"

"Sure." Herman rubbed his eyes and exhaled again. "I'll never forget it. The image is burned into my brain. It was tall, maybe eight feet or so and light-colored. It walked like a human, but it wasn't human. Its skin was papery looking." He rubbed his fingers together as if remembering how a certain texture felt. "But it wasn't made of paper."

"Corn husks," Grim offered.

"Yes!" Herman snapped his fingers. "That was how it looked, like a huge corn husk creature. Anyway, it reached the tree line and then sank onto its knees. It slithered like a snake over to the car as Newman was getting inside. I had no idea what was happening, you have to understand. I saw the *thing* open the gas door and reach its hand down into the fuel tank. The weird part is"—his voice broke—"the hand was on fire; flames were atop it. I started to yell at Newman, but the car exploded."

Herman dropped his face once more into his hands and sobbed. It was a deep, guttural sound, and my heart immediately broke for him.

But Grim was not impressed. His gaze cut to his fingers, where he appeared to study the dirt (or lack of) under his nails.

It was right after Herman released a whining sob that he asked, "And why didn't you tell anyone about the creature?"

Herman sniffled and blotted his eyes with his palms. "Who would have believed me? I saw a creature approach Newman's car. Who was going to buy that?"

He had a point. I believed him, but Grim's jaw was tight. "Had you seen anything like it before?"

"No," Herman said pointedly, "and I hope never to again. I can understand why you'd think I was lying. Given my history with Newman and all."

The hairs on the back of my neck prickled to attention. "Your history?"

"Yeah. He beat me in an essay writing competition."

"I'm sorry." I tugged on my ear to make sure it wasn't stopped up. "What did you say?"

Herman huffed and glanced skyward, seeming to resent having to explain himself. "We went to college together. Newman was in all my English classes. We were neck and neck in terms of grades, and then there was an essay contest. I was a shoo-in, or so I thought. But Newman won. We became friends after that."

"Wait." I lifted my hands in a stop motion. "I'm sorry. The two of y'all went to college?"

"Yes, what's hard to understand? Being an English major doesn't pay the bills. I had to go into another line of work. So did Newman. That's how we wound up doing the sort of business that we do."

Black market stuff, I assumed. "And what's your talent? Stanislav is a knife-wielder, and Pippa is a scent assassin. What can you do?"

Herman rubbed his hands with glee. "Watch this."

He picked up the book he was reading, *Of Mice and Men,* and closed his eyes. The next thing I knew, a window appeared in the room and through it I saw a golden field and beyond, a farmhouse and two men, one bigger and one small, walking across the field.

My jaw dropped. "You can create images from books."

Herman opened his eyes and the scene dissolved. "More than that. I can put you in the scene. You can be dropped in the middle of *The Shining.* Within a few hours you'll wind up mad."

"That's not something to brag about," Grim growled.

Herman shrugged. "It is when you get paid a lot of money to make it happen."

Grim grunted. "You have magic. But the other two assassins didn't."

"Yeah. Maybe that's why they didn't see the creature." Herman shivered. "I'd be glad never to again. But I promised that I'd stay until this case was solved." He rose and patted his chest. "But by telling you, in a way it is solved. I don't feel pressured to remain in town. So maybe I will go home."

"Pippa and Stanislav won't like it," I told him.

He cringed. "Right."

Grim rose and I followed suit. "Can you tell me exactly where the creature came from in the woods?"

"I'll even draw you a map." Herman tore a sheet of paper from a notepad provided by the motel. He drew a rough sketch of the part of the lake where we had met Newman and drew arrows indicating where the withering had come from. "That's it, right there. Think you can find it?"

Grim nodded. "Seems clear enough." He folded the paper and tucked it into his shirt pocket. "I'll head out there today and will contact you if I have any questions."

"Be careful," Herman warned. His eyes were wide as plates, and I knew that what he had seen really had scared the absolute crapola out of him. "I thought at first that the creature had died in the explosion, but when I glanced back at it, after the shock wave of energy had died down, it was slinking back off, into the night. That thing, whatever it is, is indestructible."

I shivered. It went along with what Grim and Pam had both told me about the withering. There was no known way to kill it. So how could something that was indestructible be destroyed?

I hoped Grim had an answer for that.

We thanked Herman and headed back to the car. Once inside, I mused, "Boy, what I wouldn't give for a book that could trap creatures inside."

Grim nodded. "That may be our only way to defeat the withering."

I swallowed a knot of worry that had balled up in my stomach. Not wanting to look afraid, I smiled at Grim. "At least we found out some information from Herman."

"As much of what he told us is true," he replied.

I frowned, not understanding. "What do you mean?"

Grim pushed a button, and the engine hummed to life. "What I

135

mean is, a lot of what he said seemed to be true. But I also got the sense that he was lying."

"Why would he lie?"

Grim's hazel eyes were hard as flecks of stone as he backed out of the parking lot. "That's what I'd like to know, too."

CHAPTER 22

J arrived at the cabin just as Abraham was hoisting one leg over his bike. He had dark circles under his eyes, something I hadn't noticed before.

"You okay?" I asked.

He yawned. "Yeah, just have this book that's been keeping me up at night."

I smiled with pleasure. "You're a reader, huh? When I was your age, I used to stay up late reading, too. I'd read under my covers with a flashlight on. I'd stay up so long past my bedtime that often I'd fall asleep with my face pressed to a book and then I'd wake up a line down my cheek from where it had laid against the page. Is that what happens to you?"

He skirted my gaze. "Yeah, something like that. But I'll be seeing you, Miss Paige. I've gotten Miss Cammie everything that she needs. Anything I can get for you?"

"No thanks." I resisted the urge to pat him on the head. Abraham was such a nice young kid. "I appreciate all that you do for her."

"It's no big deal. See you later."

With that, he pressed one foot to the pedal and pumped his legs, taking off down the gravel road.

Inside, I found Cammie sitting on the couch with a sleeve of crackers and an open jar of strawberry jam in front of her. She slathered gooey red jam onto a cracker and nibbled the edge.

"There's plenty of food if you're hungry."

"No, I've got to finish this book and get it off to Madeleine."

Her gaze flicked to me. "You find out anything about that Herman guy?"

"Not much, really," I said, being as honest as I could without giving out a whole bunch of details. "I'm going to lock myself inside. I'll be out in a bit."

"Ferguson's picking me up for a date. I may or may not be here when you get back."

"Y'all are still getting cozy, huh? Think that you'll stay in contact once you leave?"

She smiled wistfully. "I think so. At least I hope so."

"I hope so, too."

With that, I disappeared into my bedroom to finish the book that I'd been working on for months. I opened the file and dived right in, picking up where I left off. I was only a couple of chapters away from finishing. This was my favorite part, tying everything up and leaving the reader with a feeling of hope.

The two chapters came easily, and when I was done, I saved the file and sent it to Madeleine with a note. *I'm not sure if this will completely redeem me in the eyes of my fans, but I love this book and I hope that you do, too.*

It was late and I stretched my arms over my head and rolled my shoulders back to work the kinks from them. I exhaled hard and then rose to grab a drink from the kitchen.

The cabin was quiet. Cammie had left a little while earlier. It was dark outside, but I wasn't worried for her safety because she was with Ferguson, and he wouldn't let anything happen to her.

I had just brewed a cup of tea when Snow slid through the front door.

"Snow! I've been wondering what happened to you. I was so worried."

She glanced down at her transparent body in confusion. "Worried? It wasn't as if I could be murdered."

"No, I know." I dunked the bag of tea into the cup of hot water and watched as strands of dark tea bled into the liquid. "But I thought maybe you'd crossed over without saying goodbye."

"No," she said, eyes narrowing. "I haven't yet, and I think that I know why."

I motioned to a chair. "Sit. Tell me."

She hovered above the chair while I took a seat across from her. "At first I was confused because I didn't cross over. So I went into town and talked to some friends of mine."

"Ghosts?" Stupid question, I know. But I had to ask. "Is that who you spoke to?"

She nodded slightly. "Yes. They told me that sometimes people don't cross over until they put to right what went wrong."

I scratched my head in confusion. "What does that mean?"

"It means"—her eyelids closed tight as if she was praying extra hard for a wish to come true— "that I have to find the book, where all of this started."

"We definitely do, because there's another creature on the loose." I told her all that Herman had relayed about the withering. "We've got to find the book because more and more creatures are coming from it."

A slow smile spread across Snow's lips. "Well, you're in luck, then."

I blinked, wondering how that could be possible. "I am? How am I in luck?"

She leaned down, coming so close to me that I could see straight through her head to the other side of the room. "Because I know where the book is, and I'll take you to it."

CHAPTER 23

$\mathcal{I}$ tried calling Grim, but he didn't answer the phone. Figured. The one time I get actual information that he needs, he's not available.

But it was okay. I could use my magic if anyone tried to hurt me. This, I was certain of.

Mostly.

Snow directed me as I drove. "Turn left here." She raised her hand. "That house, on the left. This is it. You can pull over."

I slid my vehicle to a stop just across the street from a small cottage with windows framed in dark shutters. The tree-lined street was close to downtown, so the homes were stacked neatly beside one another.

My gaze flicked to the street sign, and I mumbled the name. "Magnolia. I know this street."

But I couldn't remember from where.

"That's the house," Snow told me with confidence.

"How did you find it?"

She shrugged. "I went into all the homes and started looking. I would've brought the book with me if I could, you know, carry things."

I smiled kindly. "You've done good by telling me."

The sun was sinking fast into the horizon when I exited the car. The street was quiet. Most people were inside eating dinner, I imagined. Up and down the street, windows glowed with an amber light, and the sounds of televisions playing became background noise as Snow and I approached the cottage.

The lights were on, and from outside I could hear the pounding of feet, as if a child or children were running around inside.

My stomach knotted. I hated thinking that such a dangerous book could be placed with children. What if one of them got sucked into it and wound up like Snow?

Whoever was the new owner, it was possible that they didn't realize the danger that their family could potentially be in. Well, they needed to know.

Man, I really didn't want to do this all by myself. I slid my phone from my purse and glanced at the screen, holding onto the faint hope that perhaps Grim had messaged or called me and I had missed it.

But no, my screen was black. He hadn't tried to contact me at all.

We had reached the door, and I could feel Snow's gaze, one full of expectation, weighing on me. Well, here went nothing.

I knocked on the door and heard the clomping of footsteps on the other side. A bolt unlocked, and the door opened, revealing...Abraham.

I blinked to make sure that I was seeing this correctly. "Abraham, what are you doing here?"

He shrugged. "My family's staying with Auntie Patricia."

Then it hit me how I knew the address. I'd seen it before when I'd signed the lease agreement for the cabin. It had been on the contract as Patricia's home address.

"Listen," I told him, trying to wrap my head around this information, "are your parents home?"

"No, they're at work. They'll be back later."

"Shoot. I really need to speak with them."

He leaned on the doorframe and studied me. "Maybe I can help you."

I wanted to laugh. Sure, a kid could help me with a magical book. "The only way you could help me is if you recently discovered a thick book filled with drawings of magical creatures."

He rubbed his chin. "You mean the one by the guy named Hero?"

My heart stuttered to a stop, and my eyes widened to the size of basketballs. "What did you say?"

He pushed himself off the doorframe. "Come on. I'll show you."

Snow and I followed Abraham through the house. It was nicely decorated, I couldn't help but notice, with tasteful walnut furniture polished to gleaming and light, cream-colored walls. The trim was the original brown wood. It crowned the ceiling and also framed out the windows.

Abraham led us over a tile floor to a hallway lined with plush chocolate-colored carpet. He walked to the very back and opened a cherry door. Inside was a boy's room. The bed frame was a red race car and posters of sleek cars as well as one of the band the Ramones hung on the walls. A small computer desk was pushed under a single loft bed. The computer screen glowed faintly as Abraham strolled to a chair and sat facing us.

"Why are you interested in the book?"

A thrill zipped all the way to my toes. "Can I see it?"

He shrugged. "Sure." Abraham opened a desk drawer and pulled out a book. My gaze landed on the cover, and a shriek flitted from my mouth.

"Oh my gosh. You don't know how long we've been looking for this. When did it first come to you?"

He ran a finger over the leather binding. "Several weeks ago, it showed up on my bed."

"See?" Snow said. "I told you that I'd found it."

I gave her an appreciative smile before turning back to Abraham. "And have you been playing with the book? We encountered a creature covered with eyes, and for legs it had tentacles."

The boy cringed. "That may have been my fault. I accidentally called forth one of the monsters when I was out playing. As soon as it appeared, I ran away. I didn't know what to do. Please don't tell my parents. They'll kill me."

My heart broke for him. Possessing this book was too much a burden for a child. Why had the book even picked him? "Abraham, everything that's inside of here is dangerous. The book needs to be kept in a safe place. I know that it came for you, but I was hoping that you would give it to me of your own free will."

I didn't know if that would break the book's hold on Abraham, but it was worth a shot.

He stroked the cover. "These creatures in here, I thought they were just drawings until that one came out. It scared me. A lot."

"Was that the only creature that came from the book? Were there others?" I asked, thinking that the withering could have jumped from the book as well. After all, that was the theory Grim and I were working on. No, it didn't explain why the creature had specifically targeted Newman, but I had to start somewhere.

But to my disappointment, Abraham shook his head. "No, that was the only creature that came out. After that happened, I shut the book and haven't opened it since. But if you want it, here it is. You can have it."

He slid the book in my hands, and my skin jumped at the feel of it against my flesh. The book seemed to hum with a low frequency. I hadn't noticed that the first time I held it, but perhaps that was because I hadn't possessed my powers at the time.

I clasped the book to my chest, afraid of dropping it and unleashing another creature. "Thank you," I told Abraham. "You've just saved this town from any more atrocities."

He nodded. "You're welcome. Plus, I'm glad to get rid of it. You don't know how hard it is to run a successful delivery business and also do my computer stuff."

"Computer stuff?"

"Oh, you know, hacking."

My eyebrows jumped. "Hacking?"

He waved a hand and said dismissively, "Forget I ever said that."

"Oh, okay." I thanked him again. "Now, I need to get this book into a safe pair of hands."

Abraham escorted us out, and I practically dashed to my car. Soon as Snow and I were inside, my phone rang. It was Grim.

I thumbed it to life. "You won't believe what I'm holding right now."

CHAPTER 24

*G*rim did not, in fact, believe what I was holding. He was shocked that a boy had been in possession of the book the entire time.

"How did we not know this?" he asked in a mystified voice.

"Because *magic*," I joked.

He didn't laugh, but that was fine. I was used to his grim-like behavior. "I'm on my way to the lake. Can you meet me there?"

I told him that I could.

"Can you find the place where you met Newman the other night?"

Did he think I could find the place? It was practically burned into my brain. You didn't exactly forget the one place where you witnessed a car exploding.

"Yes, I remember where it is," I said coolly. No need to go into great detail about my memory.

"I'll be there in fifteen minutes. If you beat me, just wait. And keep your car running," he said.

"Why?"

"In case the withering shows up."

A pulse of worry shot through my body. "Why would it show up, exactly?"

"Because," he said darkly, "I've set bait for it."

My handle on the phone tightened. "What do you mean, you've set bait? What sort of bait? Why are you setting bait?"

"Paige," he growled, "I can't have a dangerous creature on the loose in this town. I don't know how it got here, but I suspect either someone is controlling it, or—"

"But how could someone be controlling it?" I asked, doing my best to tamp down the knots of worry that were really working a number on my stomach.

"We don't know much about these creatures," Grim reiterated. "No one's survived an encounter long enough to say more. It's a possibility that the withering could be spelled to be controlled by a witch or wizard."

I didn't like his theory because it made me feel quite vulnerable. If someone could control a dangerous monster, what else could they do?

But instead of burying myself under a mound of worry, I sighed. "Or what? You were going to give another possibility until I interrupted you, which I am now apologizing for."

I could practically hear his face break into a smile. "There's no need to apologize. We're beyond that."

Little shivers broke out over my body and danced across my skin. "Okay. No apologies. But what's the other possibility?"

He exhaled a weighted sigh. "The other possibility is that one of the three people Newman hired *is* the withering."

My blood froze. "What did you say?"

"They are the creature, and they decided to enact their revenge on Newman that night."

"But Stanislav and Pippa said they were together."

"One of them could be covering for the other."

He was right. "And Herman said that he watched the creature slink across the ground."

"Which points the finger back at the two lovers. Either way, all three of them will be coming out to the lake tonight."

Worry shot down my spine. "They will be?"

"They will. I left messages on each of their doors, telling them that I know what they've done and to meet or else I'll go to the police."

I frowned because I was missing a step. "How do you know which rooms belonged to them? We only went to Herman's at the motel."

He sighed again, and this time the sound was full of disappointment. "I am a hunter, Paige. I may not hunt humans, but I know how to track them and push them to do things."

That made me like him just a little more. "Okay. So. What's the plan?"

"The plan is for you to give me the book and then leave."

"No," I told him. "I'll meet you at the lake, but I'm staying."

"I have Savage with me," he said.

I laughed. "Your dog? You're going to need more than him."

Grim grunted. "I'll see you soon."

With that, he hung up. *On me.* In the middle of our conversation. Okay, so maybe it wasn't exactly in the middle, but he still ended the call before I was clearly ready. But that was okay. I understood. Grim wanted to get his way and that was the end of it. He might've made my girlie parts sing, but the man had a lot to learn about relationships.

Snow sat on top of the book as I drove us out to the lake. It was a cloudless night, and moonlight splashed over the tops of the full pines and poured over the water as we drove along the road that hugged the lake.

My nerves were a jumbled mess. Would Newman's hired hands show up? What was Grim's plan if the withering appeared? And could someone be a withering and also appear human?

There was so little that anyone knew about the beast that I supposed anything was possible.

I made the turnoff, and the car's tires crunched over the gravel path. My throat shriveled as we neared. I spotted a car that was parked along the side of the road, and I instantly recognized it as Grim's.

I parked beside it and grabbed the book. "I'll come with you," Snow said.

I thanked her and we got out. The peaceful humming of insects filled the air. It should have offered some comfort, but instead their callings taunted me because it sounded like they were murmuring, *Paige, Paige.*

I shivered and hugged the book close, afraid of dropping it. I reached the clearing within moments.

But there was no sign of Grim.

That only lasted a moment, because he stepped out of the shadows with Savage by his side.

Relief washed through me. "I'm so glad you're here."

He hugged me close and pressed his mouth to my head. "Thank you for meeting me."

I handed him the book, and he quickly peeled back the cover. There was enough moonlight to see by. Grim flipped over a couple of pages and then shut the book with a snap.

"I don't need to see more." He gave me a hard nod. "I'll walk you to your car."

I folded my arms. "I'm staying."

"No, you're not."

"Grim—"

He interrupted me. "Paige, I will not have another death on my head."

I winced. "You know what happened to your parents wasn't your fault, right?"

"It was my fault." He gently cupped my arm. "Let's go."

I was about to continue arguing when a car pulled up. It was sleek and black, almost the mirror image of Newman's destroyed sedan.

Grim's entire body stiffened. "It's too late. Stay back."

I glanced around. "Where?"

"Over there." He walked me several feet behind him and placed his hands on my arms. "If anything bad happens, if the withering shows up, run. Don't look back. Run for your life."

My jaw dropped. "I'm not going to leave you," I argued. "That's not what's about to happen here."

Pain filled Grim's eyes. "Paige," he warned.

"Nothing is going to happen to me."

A shadow swept over his face, and I knew he wanted to argue it. But the car's engine came to a stop, and the most that Grim mustered was a hard nod.

"Stay back," he bit out.

I did as I was told. I wasn't interested in being harmed, but I also wasn't about to leave him flailing on his own. No way.

The car doors opened, and out stepped Stanislav and Pippa from the front and Herman from the back.

Yes, he was reading a new book.

"What's this all about?" Stanislav demanded. "You always go around taping notes to innocent people's doors?"

Grim shook his head. "One of you is guilty. And I'm going to tell you which one."

A chill coiled around my spine. Grim *knew* who Newman's killer was? Then why were all three of them here at the lake? Couldn't he just as easily have confronted the lone person? Or better yet, had Cowan arrest them?

What was I even doing here?

Grim took a menacing step forward. "The night of Newman's murder, he called the three of you out here to scare Cammie and make sure that she gave him the money."

Pippa rolled her eyes. "Tell us something we don't know."

He ignored her insufferable attitude. "Once Newman gathered the money and took it back to the car, where did he put it, exactly?"

"In the back seat," Herman said, nose still deep in the book.

"Right." Grim rubbed his chin. "But what came next is even more interesting. A creature exited the woods, the same woods that the three of you had just disappeared into. With a flame on its hand, it reached into the fuel tank and caused the engine to explode. Now, all of you had grievances against Newman, some of them pettier than others. Out of all of you, Stanislav had the most reason to want him dead—vengeance for the affair. But you, Stanislav, are already getting your revenge by your relationship with Pippa."

Stanislav shot Pippa a worried look. "Our love isn't about revenge."

"I agree," Grim said, getting all Inspector Clouseau on them.

He next turned to Pippa. "And you were angry about a contest, but that happened a long time ago. You don't seem like the type to hold on to a grudge for something so trivial."

He was narrowing down the field of suspects fast, with only one left to go—Herman. Had Herman used the withering?

"But you," Grim said, directing his attention to the bookworm. "When you mentioned the essay that you had written and that Newman had won the competition, there was something in your eyes, a burning for what you'd lost. You, whose entire life is books, you were bested by an oaf."

148

Pippa piped up. "Newman wasn't an oaf."

Stanislav smirked. "Yes, he was. Newman was an oaf."

"Oh yeah, I guess you're right," Pippa relented.

Herman lowered the book. "I'm not that petty."

"Aren't you? Aren't all of you?" Grim said. He fixed his gaze back on Pippa. "That oily stain on the bottom of your purse wasn't gasoline, like you said. It was something else. Herman came to you, said he wanted to get back at Newman, but he needed the help of both of you to make sure he got away with it. You watched while the monster stalked into the night and killed Newman. The three of you were in on it."

Pippa's face became stony. "You can't prove any of it."

"Yes, I can," Grim told them. "You'd already said that you and Stanislav were together. You were together, watching the whole thing."

Herman threw up his hands. "And what about the monster? What a joke! What sort of monster are you even talking about?"

At that, Grim's hands ignited with power. He presented the book, and my stomach fluttered as he opened the cover and a cyclone of power shot out into the night.

It extended like an arm, reaching for Herman, who threw down his novel and ran. Pippa shrieked and Stanislav grabbed her, tugging her away from the whirlwind that threatened to swallow Herman whole.

Grim infused his power into the book, causing lightning to flash and thunder to roar from the pages. Smoke curled into the sky as the pull of the pages intensified.

Worry pulsed through me. Was Grim going to pull Herman in? But there was no withering. There wasn't one creature around. What was he doing?

Savage began to growl. The hairs on his back rose to attention as he barked at Herman.

The book's magic locked on to Herman, who was fighting the pull. "You're wrong about everything," he shouted.

But as he said it, as he yelled, the fingers of his hands stretched and became a pale yellow. His legs elongated and his torso grew, giving him height that the man didn't have seconds prior.

My entire body went still with shock. It took a moment for me to process what I was seeing, because the magnitude of the horror hit me right in the gut. My mind was split between what was real and what was impossible.

It was impossible to believe that I was watching a human morph into a monster, a creature like nothing I'd ever witnessed.

Herman's eyes stretched and became inky wells of despair. His arms and legs were like scarecrow's limbs, exaggerated and grotesque. The hair that had once been brown became a crown of jagged corn husk–like tendrils that sprouted up from his skin.

There was nothing, absolutely nothing left of the man he had been standing on the ground only moments before.

Stanislav grabbed Pippa's arm. "Let's get out of here!"

They jumped into the car and drove away as the book's magic tugged on Herman.

He bowed over for a moment and then straightened with a fierce yell that held its own power. The cyclone of magic pulling on him broke, and the shock wave hit Grim and sent the book flying across the grass.

"And then there were two," Herman said in a low, guttural voice, seeming to suggest that it was only he and Grim left.

Grim's shoulders tightened. He reached behind him and pulled two blades from sheaths that had been secured under his coat.

"Let's dance, Withering," Grim said. "I'm ready to end this."

CHAPTER 25

The withering took an intimidating step forward. Just watching the creature made a chill tighten around my spine. There was nothing like it that I'd ever seen on this earth, and I had the feeling that I wouldn't see anything like it ever again.

Grim strode forward, blades raised, and I realized that at this point I could help him.

Only one person had ever fought a withering and lived. We were about to make that three.

The withering looked down at his hands, and they ignited into flames. He thrust at Grim, who attacked with his blades.

Well, Herman must've been made from a corn husk of steel, because the blades hit the withering but they did not slice through. They simply bounced off. The creature lunged for Grim with a fiery hand, but Grim spun out of his reach.

Meanwhile Savage attacked the withering, barking and biting at his feet. The creature looked down and growled, the sound sending a shiver straight to my heart.

There was nothing human in the sound.

While Grim fought, I realized the one thing that I could do was retrieve the book. I raced for it.

But just as I reached it, the withering's hand shot out and blocked my path.

"Stay away, Paige," Grim yelled.

"Come closer," the creature purred to me. "Come with me."

That, I knew, wasn't the sort of invitation that I actually wanted, so I backed off, feeling powerless.

The beast turned its head toward Grim, the movement insect-like, resembling a beetle. "You should join me," he said to Grim.

"I'm not a monster," Grim retorted, blade swinging.

"I have no weaknesses."

"Everybody's got a weakness," Grim replied, breathless. He shot a bolt of lightning at the creature, and it bounced off his skin. "I just haven't found it yet."

Herman, or whatever had taken over his body, laughed. "Join me and love the need to kill. Succumb to the darkness inside of you."

"Light destroys the darkness," Grim countered, sending another bolt shooting at his head. "You will be destroyed."

"I cannot and will not be. This is true power," he growled. "All my life, I've been made fun of, disrespected. Then a chance encounter changed me. I am all-powerful and nothing you can do will stop that."

Nothing that Grim threw at the withering affected it. Nothing. I had the sense that whatever armor covered his body, it was nearly impregnable. Perhaps we needed to crank up the wattage.

I threw out my magic. Since I'd been hanging around Grim, my power would be electrified, like him. I tossed a line of magic at the creature, hoping to hit him hard.

The magic splashed over his body, taking him by surprise. He faltered for a step, bowing back. But then he straightened, and his inky-black eyes focused on me.

"You want to play, little girl? We can play."

His stretchy arms extended from his body, lunging for me. I barely escaped before his fists punched into the ground, sending earth flying into the sky.

"I told you to stay out of it," Grim yelled.

"You need help. Nothing's working," I yelled back.

His jaw was tight, and he moved like water, slashing and turning in fluid movements. How did I *not* know that he could sword fight? This wasn't even fencing. It was hard-core slashing and thrusting.

"The book," Grim seethed.

It still lay on the ground. I threw out my magic, and a line of power coiled around the book. I pulled back my hand like I was reeling in a fishing line, and the book launched into the air. I caught it with both hands.

"To me," Grim shouted.

Savage was keeping Herman busy, lunging and biting, dodging the withering's attacks. But Herman kicked the dog, sending him skidding across the ground.

"You're going to pay for that," Grim growled.

His sheathed his swords and placed a hand on the book. His palm glowed. When he opened the book, the cyclone jumped from the pages again.

He aimed them at the withering, and the book started to pull.

Grim shot me a look fraught with worry and reluctance. "Use your magic on him. Get him into the book."

I did as he said, throwing my magic onto the monster. Sweat poured down my forehead as my power coiled around him, wrapping him up like a blanket.

The withering fought and struggled, but I held tight. Herman flexed his arms against me, but I was a witch with power, and I had more magic than I knew what to do with because it was pouring out of me.

Perhaps it was because of the great need I had in that moment. I really *had* to get that monster gone. Herman had killed once, and I knew it was only a matter of time before he did so again.

There was so much hate flowing from him that it was obvious.

My lasso of magic was working. I started to pull the withering forward, and it began to move, howling in protest.

Grim placed the book on the ground, and he threw his own power around the creature. With both of us pulling, Herman had no choice but to be dragged forward. He fought the entire way, but we were going to win this. Hope filled me to my toes.

"Get back," Grim commanded.

We each took several steps back, behind the book. The withering was only a few feet away now, and he was still grunting and struggling against the binds of magic.

"Come on," Grim said impatiently. "Get in the book."

The creature was only inches away now. I gave a hard yank, and Herman's foot touched the page. The book swallowed his foot, and he quickly dropped to his waist into the tome.

But Herman wasn't going down without a fight, and with a great show of power, he spread out his arms and broke the magic holding him. His hands rested on the ground, and he grunted and howled, attempting to pull himself out of the book.

"You will go in," Grim yelled, striding forward with his hand raised, magic swirling in his palm.

"Never!"

Herman raised one fiery corn husk hand and lunged it at Grim. Grim sidestepped the blow but stepped right into the cyclone in doing so.

The book pulled him down.

"No," I screamed.

Grim couldn't die in the pages. I rushed over but the withering had his hands on Grim. "You will perish," Herman said in a triumphant voice.

"No, I won't," Grim said.

With that, he pulled out his sword and thrust it into the withering's side. The monster, reveling in his triumph, wasn't expecting the blow.

The sword passed right into him. As he sank, Grim pushed himself from the book. He was out, standing on the ground, and the withering was sinking into the page when his hand shot up and his fiery finger sank into Grim's chest.

The withering smiled in a way that sent terror to my bones.

"Now," Herman said in a wheezing voice, "you will become what I was."

His head bowed and he sank the rest of the way into the book and the tome snapped shut.

My gaze latched on to Grim. The point where the withering had touched him was a glowing red dot that seeped out across his chest, bleeding into his clothes.

I raced over. "Grim!"

He stared at me a moment, his face full of shock. Then he stumbled back as if registering some knowledge that I wasn't privy to.

"Go home, Paige," he growled.

My brow wrinkled in confusion. "What? No. What did he do to you?"

"Just go home."

Without another word, Grim turned and walked away, heading toward his car. Savage was up by this time, and the dog padded over to him.

I wasn't going to be dismissed so easily. Not after everything that Grim and I had shared. So of course I raced after him.

"Stop! Let me help you!"

Grim had reached his car, and I touched his shoulder. He whirled around, his face tight with simmering fury.

"Paige, for your own safety, you will leave me alone."

"But what...what happened?"

He ripped open his shirt, which was something I would ordinarily have swooned over. But the red dot was gone, and in its place was a scorched mark with tentacles of inky black that looked like smudges bleeding out over his flesh.

"This," he explained, "is the infection that the withering put into me."

"What?" I said, trying to wrap my head around what he was saying. "What are you talking about?"

His eyes narrowed, resembling shards of steel. "Paige, the withering infected me."

"With what?"

"*With what it is.*" He sighed and dropped his head. When he looked up, sorrow filled his eyes. "As of right now, I will become a withering. Stay away from me. Stay far, far away, because I don't want you to be hurt."

"But—"

"Stay away," he boomed.

The anger in his voice made me stumble back. I stared at him. I knew my face was flooded with hurt. But the only emotion that came off Grim was a tight jaw.

"It's for your own good," he muttered before getting into his car.

I watched while he drove off with Savage, leaving me alone in the woods.

Well, not completely alone. Snow floated over. "I'm sorry," she said.

I nodded sadly. "I'm sorry, too. Come on. Let's get the book and go home."

CHAPTER 26

*C*ammie was back from her date by the time I returned, spent, with the book in hand. She asked how my evening had gone, and I didn't have the heart to tell her the truth about it.

I entered my bedroom and locked the door behind me. My mind swirled with so many thoughts. Grim was infected by the withering? What did that even mean? Would he slowly die? Was there a cure? I'd saved him one time from an infection. It was possible to save him again, I was sure of it.

I tried calling, but he didn't answer. My heart broke that he was pushing me away. We'd only just come together. I mean, really come together. I'd opened up to him, and he'd done the same with me, sharing painful memories—the events that made Grim the man he was. That was a man that I respected, desired and cared for deep in my bones.

It sliced my heart in two that he'd pushed me away.

I took a long breath and considered it. Tonight, emotions had been swirling. In the morning, after Grim had time to think about everything, he would realize that a cure was possible, and that we would find a way to help him together. Things would be different when a little light hit them.

He would be more open to talking.

I laid my head on my pillow and went to sleep.

The next morning, birds chirped outside my window. I'd tossed and turned for hours but had managed to eke a few moments of fitful rest from the night.

The first thing I did was check my phone to see if I'd missed any calls from Grim.

I had not.

Cammie was up and singing in the kitchen, so I peeked out.

She spotted me while she was pouring a cup of coffee. "Morning, sunshine!" I slipped into the room. My sister got a good look at me, and her eyes flared to Cracker Barrel jumbo-sized food plates. "What's wrong?"

I raked my fingers through my hair, which was stiff with dirt and debris. How had I gone to sleep without brushing it?

Shock, I supposed.

"It's a long story," I said.

She poured a second cup of coffee and pushed it toward me. "I've got some time. I'm unemployed, in case you don't remember."

I sighed, as I hadn't even processed what had happened, so I wasn't sure how to explain it to anyone else. But if anything, Cammie was a decent listener and she deserved to know the truth about what had happened to Newman, so I plopped onto the couch and filled her in.

"So it was Herman all along," she mused. "Son of a gun. The little dweeb was the one behind it all along."

I nodded. "Yep. It was him. He was a horrible, terrible monster who killed Newman and would have gone on to harm others. He said something about having the urge to kill."

I dropped my face into my hands as thoughts of Grim filled my head. Cammie gently shook my shoulder. "What is it?"

"Before Herman got sucked into the book, he infected Grim with the same disease that turned him into a monster."

She cringed. "Infected him? So now he's going to become a monster?"

"I don't know."

"Well, you'd better get over there and see what's going on."

She was right. Sitting here wasn't doing me any good. "I'll do it!"

I jumped up and quickly showered and dressed, grabbing a cup of coffee to go on my way out the door. Cammie asked if I wanted her to go with me, but I said no. The one thing I did take, however, was the book. It could help him. I didn't know how, but maybe it would assist Grim.

I arrived at his house within minutes, and instead of knocking politely, I pounded on the door. I didn't hear Grim shuffling inside and was about to turn and leave when the door flew open.

He looked gloriously beautiful with his hair hanging in waves around his face and his golden skin gleaming in the sun. His cheeks and chin held a day of scruff on them, and I wanted to run my fingers over their sandy texture. But as much as I wanted to wrap my arms around his waist and inhale his scent, his eyes were a barrier. The beautiful jewel tones were hard chips of stone.

I swallowed a lump in my throat. "Hey."

"What are you doing here?" he asked gruffly.

I would not be intimidated by his harsh attitude. He was hurting. I knew that. His go-to was to push those who cared about him away when his heart ached. He wouldn't do that to me, though.

"What I'm doing here is helping you," I told him.

He sighed and glanced off into the distance. His jaw jumped in a way that I knew meant he was annoyed, but I wasn't going anywhere. Grim didn't get to invite me into his life and then shut me out without telling me.

"Come in," he said grudgingly.

I followed him into the house. Savage padded up and placed his nose under my hand in welcome. I bent down and scratched behind his ears.

"He's okay?" I asked Grim.

Grim grunted. Of course. Standard reply when he was annoyed.

I rose and held out the book. "I brought this for you. Thought you might want to keep it."

He quirked a brow but kept his distance. "It may just disappear and return to its owner."

"It might." I shrugged. "But it might not since you used it." My gaze roved to the spot on his chest where the withering had touched him. Grim wore a T-shirt, making it impossible to see if the mark was still there.

"I've still got it," he gruffed.

My gaze darted to his, and he was watching me steadily. Grim had caught me eyeing the spot on him, and he looked none too pleased that I had homed in on it.

"What are you going to do about it?"

He rolled his shoulders back and said in a terse voice, "There is practically no literature on witherings. What there is, is very little. Most of it is told to others, legends, as it were. I don't know how to save myself, and as far as I know, I will become one."

My heart sliced in two. I crossed to him and hugged him. Whether he wanted it or not, Grim was getting a full-fledged hug from me.

"We can heal you," I breathed into his chest. "We will find a way."

Then Grim's hands were on my arms, but he wasn't returning the embrace. He gripped me gently and pressed me back with his brute man strength. I tipped my face up to him, my expression asking, *Why? Why are you pushing me away?*

"Paige, you cannot be near me. I can't be near anyone. I'm becoming a monster, whether I like it or not. This thing that Herman put inside of me, it's growing."

"But I can't lose you. I only just found you." My heart tightened and I nearly said that I loved him, but I held back.

I wiped away a tear that slid down my cheek. "What are you going to do?"

He ground his teeth. "I'm going to search out the truth. Try to find answers. But I'm doing it alone."

"No," I cried.

Pain twisted his face. He looked down at me, and his eyes burned with emotion. He didn't want to leave; I could see that much. But as quickly as the emotion flared brightly in his eyes, it vanished and was replaced with a stoic coldness that chilled my heart.

"If I stay," he said gently, running a hand over my hair, "I will kill you. I will kill anyone and everyone. Herman was not lying—there is a lust for death and destruction in this, and I feel it wanting to take over every part of me."

He pressed his lips to my forehead, and I curled my fingers into his shirt.

"Stay," I said, my voice desperate. A girl didn't want to plead, but I had only just found Grim. He couldn't go. "I can help you."

"No, you can't." He took my hands and untangled my fingers from his shirt. "One day you'll understand that I'm doing this for you. Because I..."

My gaze darted to his eyes, searching. "Because you what?"

Emotion flashed over his face, and his jaw jumped as he bit down on whatever feeling was warring inside of him. "Goodbye, Paige."

He took a step toward his couch, and that was when I spotted the duffel bag sitting on the cushion. He plucked a set of keys from a table. "These are the keys to the house. Ferguson's going to take them and watch over the greenhouse. But if you want to, you can."

He was giving me a part of him, a tiny consolation prize, and for that I was ticked. "I don't want them," I said coldly.

He nodded as if understanding why I'd made that choice. "Come, Savage."

The dog padded over to him, and Grim took me in one last time. I took him in, and a world of words clotted up my throat. Our story was just beginning; how could he let it end this way?

"It's for the best," he said as if trying to convince himself more than me.

I couldn't even respond. I dropped my head and closed my eyes, listening as he walked toward me and then paused beside me for a brief moment. I thought for sure he would say something or decide to stay because it was so stupid for him to leave.

But he didn't. He kept walking until the door shut and he was gone.

I listened as his car started and he pulled out of his driveway. When he was down the road, I took a deep inhale and surveyed his house.

He'd called me his muse, and I wanted to see what his feelings for me had created, at least one last time.

I entered the greenhouse to a buzz of creatures. I couldn't see them, but I could hear them. Light pierced the leaded glass and poured over the palms and other vegetation. Mist from the waterfall filled the room, and I walked toward the pool, passing the bookcase filled with magical books.

One of these probably had the answer to heal Grim inside of it. But he was being so pigheaded that he didn't see it.

I felt abandoned, alone. But in that moment, all that helplessness washed away. I knew what I was supposed to do.

I was going to help Grim whether he liked it or not.

I pushed my shoulders back, crossed to the bookcase, and grabbed the first tome I could find that suggested it held healing spells.

I laid it on a table, cracked its spine back and started to read.

EPILOGUE

*I*n the weeks that passed, I texted Grim nearly every day. He never responded, which wasn't a surprise. I also watched over his house, wanting to be as close to him as possible, even though he was gone.

Cammie also got herself together and made decisions about what would come next for her. "Well, sis," she said. "I'm all packed up. You promise that you're going to visit?"

"Of course." I gave her a big hug as we stood outside, waiting for her ride to arrive. "Ferguson's taking you home?"

She smiled. "Yep. He sure is. Said he wants to see my life. Maybe we can work things out together, see where they go."

"That's great," I replied, meaning it.

She hugged me again, and she smelled of vanilla and roses. I loved her smell; it reminded me of comfort. She released me and patted my back.

"You call anytime, okay?"

"Scout's honor," I said, lifting my first two fingers in pledge. "I will."

Ferguson pulled up. Cammie shot me a wide smile. "I'll call you, okay? And hey, you let me know if you hear anything from Grim."

My heart tightened at his name, but I said, "I will. Of course."

The love that I felt for him (yes, it was love—I knew that) hadn't burned away. In fact, it had grown as I entered his greenhouse every day and watered the plants and learned about the creatures.

I often wondered if he loved me too, and deep down I thought that he did. That was why he'd left, and I couldn't be angry with him for that.

I hugged Cammie one last time and was happy that we'd come to an understanding. We might not completely understand one another, but we were sisters and shared a bond.

They drove away and I stood for moment, watching the dirt from the road lift into the sky.

My phone rang and my heart seized. It wasn't Grim, however. It was Madeleine.

"Paige, darling, how are you?"

"I'm...fine," I replied, hesitating. No need in saying the truth—that I was lovesick and heartbroken.

"Great. Listen, we're on for a publication date. Are you ready? Your publicist wants to book a tour and signings."

I sighed. "Madeleine, that isn't what I want anymore. I just want a quiet book release, and if that means it doesn't do as well, so be it. But I've gotten used to a quiet life and I just don't have all of that in me anymore."

Madeleine paused. After a few seconds she replied, "Of course, darling. You were so burned last time, I get it. I'll tell them. And to be honest, I don't think it'll matter because this book is great. Best thing you've ever written."

"Thanks," I told her.

We hung up and I stood outside for another moment watching as the sun started to slink into the horizon. I glanced over my shoulder into the cabin's window and spotted the empty living room. Snow had crossed to the other side not long after everything that happened with the withering. I was sad not to have her company, but relieved that she'd found the peace she deserved.

My phone bleeped and I expected it to be Madeleine with a follow-up, so I casually glance down and nearly dropped the phone.

It was Grim.

He'd texted. My finger trembled as I slid it across the glass to unlock the screen. I pressed the text app, and his name screamed at me.

I opened his message, holding my breath, afraid of what he had to say.

But it was only two words.

My muse.

But that was all I needed to feel hope. It was also all I needed for one other thing. I left the message and pulled up a number. The phone rang several times before he finally picked up.

"Miss Cammie?"

"Abraham, do you have a second?"

"Sure thing. What can I do for you?"

My stomach tightened, but here went nothing. "Listen, do you think that you can find the location that a text was sent from?"

"Maybe. It's on your phone?"

"Right."

"Let me see it and I'll tell you."

I smiled. "I'll be right there."

Where is Grim? Will he be saved from the withering infection growing inside of him?
Find out in his own limited series. The first book, GRIM, is on sale now.

BUY GRIM

If you never want to miss a release, be sure to sign up for my newsletter. You'll have access to sneak peaks of books and will be notified whenever I'm running a sale! Click HERE.

And join my private Facebook Group, the Bless Your Witch club. There, we chat about books and get to know one another. You'll get to do fun things like vote on covers and read unedited chapters. You'll be the first to know insider info. You can join HERE.

ALSO BY AMY BOYLES

MAGICAL DAMES AND DATING GAMES

SOME PIG AND A MUMMY DIG

SWEET TEA WITCH MYSTERIES

SOUTHERN MAGIC

SOUTHERN SPELLS

SOUTHERN MYTHS

SOUTHERN SORCERY

SOUTHERN CURSES

SOUTHERN KARMA

SOUTHERN MAGIC THANKSGIVING

SOUTHERN MAGIC CHRISTMAS

SOUTHERN POTIONS

SOUTHERN FORTUNES

SOUTHERN HAUNTINGS

SOUTHERN WANDS

SOUTHERN CONJURING

SOUTHERN WISHES

SOUTHERN DREAMS

SOUTHERN MAGIC WEDDING

SOUTHERN OMENS

SOUTHERN JINXED

SOUTHERN BEGINNINGS

SOUTHERN MYSTICS

SOUTHERN CAULDRONS

SOUTHERN HOLIDAY

SOUTHERN ENCHANTED

SOUTHERN TRAPPINGS

THE ACCIDENTAL MEDIUM

WITCH'S BLOCK

POISONED PROSE

SPELL, DON'T TELL

SOUTHERN GHOST WRANGLER MYSTERIES

SOUL FOOD SPIRITS

HONEYSUCKLE HAUNTING

THE GHOST WHO ATE GRITS (Crossover with Pepper and Axel from Sweet
Tea Witches)

BACKWOODS BANSHEE

MISTLETOE AND SPIRITS

BLESS YOUR WITCH SERIES

SCARED WITCHLESS

KISS MY WITCH

QUEEN WITCH

QUIT YOUR WITCHIN'

FOR WITCH'S SAKE

DON'T GIVE A WITCH

WITCH MY GRITS

FRIED GREEN WITCH

SOUTHERN WITCHING

Y'ALL WITCHES

HOLD YOUR WITCHES

SOUTHERN SINGLE MOM PARANORMAL MYSTERIES

The Witch's Handbook to Hunting Vampires

The Witch's Handbook to Catching Werewolves

The Witch's Handbook to Trapping Demons

ABOUT THE AUTHOR

Hey, I'm Amy,

I write books for folks who crave laugh-out-loud paranormal mysteries. I help bring humor into readers' lives. I've got a Pharm D in pharmacy, a BA in Creative Writing and a Masters in Life.

And when I'm not writing or chasing around two kids (one of which is seven going on seventeen), I can be found antique shopping for a great deal, getting my roots touched up (because that's an every four week job) and figuring out when I can get back to Disney World.

If you're dying to know more about my wacky life, here are three things you don't know about me.

—In college I spent a semester at Marvel Comics working in the X-Men office.

—I worked at Carnegie Hall.

—I grew up in a barbecue restaurant—literally. My parents owned one.

If you want to reach out to me—and I love to hear from readers— you can email me at amyboylesauthor@gmail.com.

Happy reading!

Printed in Great Britain
by Amazon

20071409R00103